SUBURBAN

GOTHIC

Margaret F. Chen

Printed through Opus Self-Publishing Services
Located at:
Politics and Prose Bookstore
5015 Connecticut Ave. NW
Washington, D.C. 20008
www.politics-prose.com / / (202) 364-1919

CONTENTS

One Saturday afternoon, Mark and Annie Zhang decided to visit their tenants, Frank and Naomi Olivetti, to see for themselves the purportedly amazing landscaping work the Olivettis had completed over the past few months, as reported by one of their former neighbors, Mrs. Winifred Callahan. Mrs. Callahan had initially contacted Mark and Annie about a downed maple she had insisted, quite rightly, that the Zhangs remove from her yard after a windstorm knocked it down from the Olivetti/Zhang side. This the Zhangs accomplished with upstanding alacrity, hiring the EZ Tree Company whose phone number and reputation ("expensive but good") Mrs. Callahan had conveniently furnished, along with an unsolicited update on the Olivettis.

The Olivetti's numerous yard projects were not a surprise to Annie as Naomi had asked permission to start these months ago, and then followed up with a series of letters, informing the Zhangs of their progress. *Stop by any time*, Naomi had written in her small, neat cursive. *We'd love to show you what we've done.* Annie had assured her that they most certainly would. Rockville *was* on the Maryland side—they were now on the Virginia side—and only twenty-five miles away. But one thing after another had

1

occurred that spring—Annie's grandfather passing away, a friend's wedding, work deadlines—and it had been impossible to get away. It was now late summer, and driving down the familiar, narrow road, dark as late evening due to the massive, old oaks lining the streets, Annie felt nauseated and her heart raced, as if it wanted to escape from her body. She said to Mark, "It's so dark here. I don't remember it being this dark, not at three in the afternoon."

Mark, who soon after their marriage had begun to automatically disagree with his wife on almost everything, remarked mildly, "It's always been like this. At least, in the summer." Annie wanted, all of a sudden, more than anything, to turn around and go home. But they had come all this way already, had been stuck on the Beltway for an hour and a half earlier, and there was no way Mark—or Annie, either, for that matter—was going through *that* ordeal again.

So here they were, driving through their old neighborhood, past the same seedy strip malls, the favorite Safeway, the well-known bend in the road, and the railroad tracks they had bumped over time and time again (and if they turned right instead of going straight, they could drive to the air-conditioned, glass-towered bookstore at White Flint Mall, where readers could sit unconflicted, quiet, and absorbed in their own worlds, not bothering anyone…if only they could go *there* instead). But instead, down their old street, Ruby Drive, they went. And up ahead, a gigantic white clapboard house, with a mismatched third-story red-brick addition, loomed over their own smaller rental. The unwieldy clapboard belonged to the Zumans. Although she tried to stop herself, Annie began to fix her gaze upon the large house, as if a magnetic force gravitated forth from its many black windows, pulling her very eyeballs, it seemed, right out of their sockets and towards the walls of staring, glassy recesses. She had expected the Zuman children to be running around, but there was not a person in the yard, near the house, or on the streets.

Mark and Annie's rental—the first home they had ever purchased, and which they had lived in for less than a year—was like many of the other single-story, three-bedroom brick ranches on the street—compact, solid, with pale green shutters, a tiny carport, and a long, sloping driveway. Inside, the rooms were spacious, light-filled, with shiny hardwood floors. There was a full-sized, half-finished basement, and a new washer and dryer in the laundry room by the stairs. Outside, a small stone patio faced a broad, shaded backyard. The real estate agent had called it "cute"—a starter home—and Annie had dreamed of all the gardening projects she would start once they settled in. But then she had met the Zumans—and had found herself going out into the yard less and less. The Zuman's overbuilt, decrepit Colonial gave her the creeps. A dilapidated chain-link fence, covered in weeds and leaning against muddy heaps of old bicycles, rusting lawn chairs, and plastic toys, inadequately separated the

Zuman's yard from the Zhang's. Inside the house, Annie had mostly kept the shades lowered on the Zuman side. Once or twice she had defiantly opened them, but that had lasted only a few hours—maybe it had been her imagination, but there was the feeling, this crawling sensation, that beyond the mess of blackberry bushes, beyond the fence, behind those dark windows, someone—something—was staring out at her, spying, perhaps, not only into the privacy of her home, but into the very depths of her carefully-guarded soul.

Annie never thought she was one to be intimidated by a mere family from the burbs, even one with a lot of children and a thrash-strewn yard. The yard, after all, had been in approximately the same unattractive condition when Annie and Mark first started looking at their own house next door, but Annie had chosen, in the excitement of possibly finding their "perfect" home, to ignore the weeds, the rusty fence, the junk peeking over the fence. While researching the neighborhood, she had learned the schools weren't that great. But she and Mark had no children yet and were not planning to have any. The realtor, when asked about the neighbors, had not known anything or pretended not to know, and the former owners, betraying only the slightest hesitation, commented briefly that the Zumans had "a lot of kids" but that everyone was "very nice." As if to dispel any doubts, Mrs. Zuman, plump, smiling, grandly adorned in a flowing, turquoise and burnt-orange house dress, trailing a pungent perfume of deep-fried foods, ambled over during one of the Zhang's first visits—they had been pondering over the pros and cons of the carport—and welcomed them with a gap-toothed grin and a gentle—or one might alternatively say, tepid—handshake. This small gesture convinced Annie that the Zumans were, indeed, perfectly nice, friendly people, a perfectly nice family.

But the Zumans were not just any family, Annie learned soon enough. They were a very large, extroverted, mixed-race family: exotic, street-wise, and a permanent, well-known fixture to the Ruby Drive neighborhood. Annie had always believed she had a particular affinity for mixed-race families, being from one herself (although she would never consider herself extroverted, exotic, or street-wise). Annie's father was German and her mother Chinese. Mr. Zuman, Annie learned from Mrs. Zuman, was part Swedish and part Thai, and Mrs. Zuman herself was Pakistani. Branching out from this main line were seven kids, ranging in ages from nine to twenty-five, two maternal grandparents, and a Rottweiler. After meeting Mrs. Zuman, Annie started seeing the messy yard in a different light—the untidiness became charming, and she felt sympathetically towards the overgrown house next door with its accompanying overgrown weeds, much as she would feel towards a large, clumsy child. In any case, wasn't she, Annie, an inveterate collector of things as well? She hated throwing anything out, and had spent numerous hours, if not months or even years, sorting through piles of newspapers, old clothes, old papers, drawerfuls of knick-knacks, just so she wouldn't miss anything of use. All of that organizing, she reminded herself, took time, and maybe the Zumans with their sprawling family and busy lives just didn't have the time to sort through things.

The seven children, all of whom she would eventually meet, were, in ascending order, Cissy, Mickey, Sydney, Wendy, Thorvald, Jeremy, and Marie. Annie did not often see the older siblings around— Marie, Thorvald, and Jimmy were in their early twenties, Sydney and Wendy in their late teens—for they quite naturally had better things to do than hang around their nerdy, housebound next-door neighbor. Sometimes she would hear voices in the backyard or outside in the driveway, people coming and going, cars revving up, zooming away, sputtering back, doors slamming. She did not often see the older children, but she heard them, that was for sure.

On the other hand, nine-year-old Cissy and eleven-year-old Mickey made frequent appearances at the Zhang's house, at least in the beginning. On the pair's first visit, both had hung back, shy and uncertain, all of which Annie found understandable and endearing, having been a shy child herself. But she soon discovered that timidity was not their natural disposition. Cissy, a pretty girl, with long, dark-brown hair, large, green eyes and dry, brown skin, a little on the plump side, immediately began running her hands along the Williams Sonoma tablecloth—the fidgety type, Annie decided—and wanted to know the price of the sofa, the television, the Depression-glass collection. Mickey, a smaller, jauntier boy-version of Cissy, asked about Mark's chess set, and remarked that the African masks and hunting spears hanging on the wall were "cool." Annie, amused by their curiosity, chalked up the lack of restraint to naive over-enthusiasm. She doubted they would come back to visit again, as grown-up possessions—and grown-ups, in general—were probably boring to kids like Cissy and Mickey. Or so Annie thought.

Because back again they were the next day. Annie offered cookies and iced tea, while Mickey inspected the stereo system and tried out, to Annie's embarrassment, several of her CDs. Neither he nor Cissy had heard of ABBA or the Beatles, Bach or Beethoven, but even as they made faces and giggled at the music, Cissy declared that she liked "The Moonlight Sonata" and "Strawberry Fields." Annie glowed with all the aura of good influence, envisioning herself as a surrogate mother-teacher, perhaps—she would instruct these ignorant children in music, in science, in literature, she would take them on outings to museums and concerts. Cissy then asked if they could stay and watch television. Annie said no, she had some work to do that afternoon. Mickey asked if he could borrow the spears, to which Annie also said no. She asked if they would like her to show them how to play chess on Mark's marble set, and they said yes, but after struggling through an overly complicated explanation of each of the pieces, they grew bored and began kicking at each other under the table.

"I have to work now," Annie said finally, "maybe you can stop by another day?" The children sulkily departed.

In time, only Cissy continued showing up. "Hi," she would say, "I was just coming by to visit." Again, there was that shy or furtive air, some nervous hair-pulling, but after a cookie or two, she would quickly settle into her usual cross-legged position on the braided rug, and Annie and Cissy—Annie had come to think of themselves as the "girls"—would commence their conversation. Subjects were random and varied, but questions focused primarily upon practical matters.

"How much did you pay for that?" Cissy would ask. Or: "I bet you could get twenty dollars for that." Once she asked how much the house cost (which Annie answered) and how much money Mark made (which Annie did not.) Sometimes, Annie would help Cissy with her math or spelling homework, since Cissy usually chose to come right after school.

"It's always noisy at our house," she complained. "I can't concentrate. Can I come here? It's so quiet."

Annie readily agreed. But it was hard to get any work done while Cissy was there. She would either ask questions incessantly or stare at Annie with those large, pale-green eyes.

Then there was the issue with the dog. The dog just made things phenomenally worse—for it was always barking, barking, barking. When Annie saw how he was treated, she understood why—he was kept chained in the backyard, night and day, next to the fence dividing their properties. Unfortunately, he could see right through the living room window into a large portion of the Zhang's house. Many times she looked up from her laptop to see him straining against his leash, ready to start barking at the slightest provocation—and there were plenty of affronts to set him off: if she looked out the window too long, if she took out the trash, if she tripped on the rug. All these mistakes incited him to a frenzied barking that could be heard at least three blocks away, and which sometimes lasted an entire afternoon. After a while he'd grow bored again and settle down, moping, next to his ramshackle doghouse, a pile of boards so shabby even he refused to inhabit it. The Zumans never seemed to take him inside unless he was making a particularly insane fuss. Sometimes Annie did see the kids unchain him for what she assumed was "exercise." Teasing and shouting, the kids would chase and slap him around and around the yard, up and down the street, and all over the neighborhood. Usually he ended up chasing the screeching kids back to the house. After the Zhangs moved, Mrs. Callahan told them the dog had been seized by the police and surrendered to the Montgomery County Humane Society after he was caught chasing some

9

children visiting the neighborhood. There had also been rumors about the dog terrorizing an elderly woman out for a roll in her wheelchair one day. But then the Zumans just got another dog.

No doubt, the Zumans were a mystery, and Annie never did find out some very basic information about them, such as where Mr. Zuman worked, or why all the older kids were still at home, and what they all did with their time. Annie recalled Cissy saying that one of her siblings—probably Marie, the eldest and most responsible-looking—was studying to be a nurse and attended night classes at the community college. But then, there were the other kids. She couldn't help noticing that although the Zumans didn't seem to be exactly wealthy—if the state of their home and yard could be any real indication—the older siblings did dress fashionably and drive late-model cars. Cissy informed Annie two of her brothers worked at a "club" and "made lots of money." That, at least, explained all the vehicles pulling up into their driveway late at night, accompanied by loud male voices and goonish guffaws. When Annie peeked out the blinds, there would be Thorvald and Jimmy, the two eldest brothers, swaggering around with their leather-jacketed friends.

It also did not help Annie's information-gathering mission that Cissy, the main go-between, was a chronic liar. She lied constantly. She lied for no reason. If Annie mentioned a story about an acquaintance of hers, Cissy always knew who the person was or someone else who knew the person. Annie made up someone once, just to test her, and sure enough, Cissy knew the pretend-person. Once Mickey prank-called Annie, and then he and Cissy both vigorously denied it, even though Annie's Caller ID clearly showed that the call came from their house. Annie started finding fast-food wrappers and soda cans in the yard, near the Zuman's fence. She'd storm over to the startled Mrs. Zuman, waving the garbage angrily, and Mrs. Zuman would always fake-apologize. When the prank calls started up again—this time peppered with all manner of choice words—Annie called the police. She felt a little queasy when the policewoman showed up and started questioning the Zumans, but it had to be done. This time the grandfather came over to apologize (for real, it appeared this time), and added without any relish that Mickey and Cissy were going to be "punished." Cissy would say to Annie after each similar skirmish, "I cried after you said that," but Annie didn't believe her. Cissy wasn't the crying type.

At times, Annie's own behavior, she was embarrassed to admit, went over-the-top. Once she had spotted a small pyramid of dog excrement in the middle of their front lawn. Annie managed to work herself into a rage over this, for of course it belonged to that dog of theirs, purposefully placed there by the bratty kids; somehow Annie convinced Mark, after he came home from work that day (he usually missed out on all the excitement, being at the office during the troublesome afternoon hours) to go out and take pictures of the offending pile as "evidence." He went out into the yard—in sync with Annie on this for once—armed with his old Minolta and shot twenty or so photos of the poop at various angles. Mrs. Zuman, when informed of what had happened, sent over Mickey and his school friend to clean up the mess in the end, which they did, giggling the entire time. When it was finally clear that Mark and Annie weren't going to win the battle—and that the Zumans had no intention of ever leaving their ever-growing home (another addition was being planned, behind their garage), Annie decided it was time to leave. That was when they found Frank and Naomi through a classified ad which Annie had placed in the paper. She reduced the rent, in order to be able to leave more quickly, and had received a torrent of responses. Naomi and Frank were among the first to call. When she and Mark moved out quietly one Monday, the only person who knew was Mrs. Callahan next door. But then Mrs. Callahan always knew everything.

It was now seven months since they had last handed the keys to the Olivettis, and Annie had heard not a word of complaint about the Zumans. Instead, Naomi described the new projects she and Frank were working on around the house, in beautifully hand-written letters enclosed with the rent checks. Annie had already concluded, when she had first met the Olivettis, that they would be able to deal with the Zumans much more successfully than she and Mark ever could—Naomi's letters reinforced this view even more strongly. The Olivettis were both computer programmers, like Annie (Mark was an office manager for a computer company, which was at least not so distantly related), and she was excited when Naomi showed up at their first visit, carrying exactly the same kind of black leather Coach briefcase that Annie owned. *It's a sign*, she thought to herself. She had, in addition, liked Naomi's look—the dark jeans and white, collared shirt, rolled up at the sleeves, her mass of wavy, dark hair, bright eyes, and thin, friendly face. And she had liked Frank's look (maybe even better than she liked Mark's "look")—handsome, strong features, and an open and friendly expression, just like Naomi. They went well together. She couldn't imagine these two disagreeing with each other on anything. She liked that Naomi drove a sporty little red Miata, and that Frank had a cool red and black Yamaha motorcycle. She, of course, liked how quickly they both wanted to take the house, how efficiently Naomi filled out the application, without leaving any blank spaces. Annie, somewhere in the back of her mind, knew that she and Mark were very, very lucky, especially as they had never been landlords before, and had never wanted to be. The lowered rent had something to do with it, true, but wasn't it terribly ironic, Annie mused to him after the Olivettis left, that Frank and Naomi were just like a hipper, more extroverted version of she and Mark? Of course, Mark snorted and didn't agree.

Annie learned from Naomi's letters that they had painted some of the rooms, expanded the patio, and planted shrubs. But she didn't really know what to expect.

It wasn't a surprise to see a big dent already on the driver's side of the Zuman's brand-new white SUV, parked along the curb. Their rental house didn't look the same, however. Pansies and hostas lined the driveway, and the azaleas were trimmed. Rakes and brooms were organized neatly against the side of the house. There was even a brand-new mailbox.

"Wow. Look at that," Annie pointed to Mark. "They've only been here a short while and they've got a new mailbox already. I should've given them the one we bought." Annie had also purchased a new mailbox while they lived at the house, but it had sat in the basement until they moved. She didn't remember what happened to it after that.

Naomi greeted Annie and Mark at the doorway. She looked as neat and crisply efficient today—wearing a blue Oxford shirt with jeans and straw sandals—as she had when Annie last remembered her.

"I'll show you around," Naomi said, already halfway down the hall. There were framed photos everywhere, expensive-looking throw rugs, and a white-leather sectional with several large, brightly-colored pillows. The walls had been painted softer, finer hues—a pale mauve in one room, antique gold in another. The spare bedroom which had served as a sort of storage/junk room/office while Annie and Mark had been there was now transformed into a—spare bedroom. Annie wanted to cry when she saw it. It had always been so dark, uncomfortable, and crowded while she and Mark had lived there, but now, here was a little iron bed with quilts, a braided rug, an antique dresser, and a milk-glass reading lamp. The shades Annie had always kept shut because they faced the Zuman's house were now thrown open, flooding the room with delightful, warm, leafy-green sunlight. It didn't seem to matter anymore if the Zumans were looking in or not. Perhaps that was the most striking thing of all—all the curtains and shades in the entire house facing the Zuman's side were wide open, and not just in the spare bedroom. This one difference had transformed the house, made it more agreeable-looking, open, and cheerful than Annie had ever seen. The ambiance while she and Mark had been there, she reflected now, seemed positively suspicious, dark, and distrustful.

"Can you believe this?" Annie whispered to Mark, as they walked through rooms that had once been theirs. Actually, the rooms were still theirs—and yet, she felt as if they had never really belonged here, or the house hadn't ever belonged to them. They hadn't really *known* how to live in this house. Mark shrugged. He wasn't impressed with the changes. Frank was outside on the patio, in jeans and a white T-shirt, drinking coffee and reading the paper. He smiled and stood up when he saw Annie.

"Did you do this by yourselves?" Mark asked, indicating the patio. It had been expanded to twice its former size.

Frank nodded. "The dirt came in handy for grading around the storm windows," he explained, as if it were the most logical thing in the world. Annie thought, *Mark and I would have just dumped the dirt somewhere in the woods.* If they would have even started a patio project in the first place. Which wasn't likely.

Maybe because they stood there, so awkwardly unbelieving, Frank offered gently, "Here. I'll show you." The Zhangs followed him to the side of the house which faced the Zumans. Annie had rarely spent time in this part of the yard. Now there was a little gravel path, bordered by new flowers and shrubs. And, indeed, the area around the storm windows, which had always been susceptible to puddling after storms, sloped away neatly with the new dirt.

If the inside of the house was remarkable, the landscaping outside could only be described as stunning. Annie was flabbergasted with the amount of work that must have been put into it—and Frank and Naomi had lived there only a few months.

"Roses!" Annie exclaimed. She had heard how much work they took. The ones here in the new garden were huge, healthy, bursting with color. The rose beds themselves had been carefully weeded and raked. Besides roses, there were blue hydrangeas, day lilies, baby irises, little beds of marigolds and pansies, several varieties of ferns and hostas, and other plants and flowers Annie did not recognize. New brick borders curved around the larger flower beds. The many formerly overgrown bushes and shrubs had all been neatly trimmed. A small, curved footbridge was placed far in the back, in a shady part of the yard near the woods, with stones set underneath and tiny solar lamps along the path. A set of clean, white wicker furniture was arranged on the patio, next to an expensive gas grill. There was a bird feeder next to the patio. The entire backyard had been transformed from an overgrown and neglected jungle (natural-looking, Annie had always said to herself) to a gardener's paradise—what she, in fact, had always wanted to create.

"I can't believe this," Annie kept repeating, and then, when Naomi came outside to join them, she said, almost sadly." We should give you guys the house!" Naomi laughed, a good-natured laugh, which caused Annie to feel even sadder. Mark and Frank hadn't gotten far from the patio and were discussing something obviously related to the Zumans. They were both facing the other house and pointing to it occasionally. Annie wanted to hear. She had glanced over briefly a few times while looking around outside and had felt there was something different about their yard, although she hadn't identified what—she had been too busy taking in everything in their own yard. She could hear children's voices from a far part of their yard she could not see. She could also see the Zumans' new dog, which was out, too. It was just as ugly as the first one. But this one wasn't barking at all. It wasn't even looking at Annie, but in the direction of the children's voices.

"I was just telling Mark about a burglary over at the Zumans," Frank said. "They were even home when it happened." Apparently, someone had tried to climb through an unlocked basement window one night. Before the person could make it all the way in, however, someone inside had heard the noise, and the intruder had run away.

"The funny thing is that Alexander didn't even bark when it happened," Naomi said, shrugging and smiling. "Didn't even care."

"Alexander?"

"Their new dog. He's really very nice. Never barks."

Annie looked over at Alexander, who was sitting quietly and wagging his tail. She and Mark had never even known the name of the first dog.

"So, you haven't had any problems with them?" Mark asked skeptically, crossing his arms over his chest. "The kids used to throw stuff into our yard."

"I think they did at first. We just threw it back."

As the four of them looked over, Annie realized what had given her the impression of change in the Zuman's yard—a cheap, white plastic outdoors dining set, which had definitely not been there before, was arranged on the deck; the deck, which had once been buried under a small mountain of assorted junk was now swept clean. The chairs and bicycles that used to lean against the fence had been removed. The lawn was mown. There were pink flowers along the side of the house. All this had happened after she and Mark had left. After Naomi and Frank had moved in. *The Zumans must like them*, Annie thought, and in spite of herself, she felt jealous.

"They are a little different," Naomi said, "But actually they've been pretty nice. We've met Cissy and Mickey. And they've done some landscaping recently."

"Yes, I noticed," said Annie. "Who was it, who did all that?"

"The oldest son." *Thorvald?* Annie thought incredulously. The delinquent? The one who used to swagger around at midnight? "The really tall one," Naomi went on, when Annie didn't reply, "He lifts weights, I think." Yes, that was Thorvald all right. Thorvald planting pink flowers. Annie just could not picture it. It was ludicrous. Or was it?

"It must be you two," Annie said finally. "They never did anything like that while we were here. You two must be a good influence." Her head was beginning to spin again, like it did when she and Mark had been driving up the street earlier, but this time, it was a different kind of sickness, a different kind of nausea. She was thinking that, maybe she hadn't really *seen* the Zumans, all that clearly. Maybe they hadn't known how to make their yard look better, maybe they had needed people like the Olivettis to motivate them.

She, after all, had once wanted to plant a beautiful garden, too, in this very yard. What had happened?

As she mulled over the inexplicable flowers by the fence—which was still rusty and falling apart, but at least cleared of weeds and debris—she thought back to the time, although it had been a very brief one, when she and Mark had first moved in, when she hadn't been bothered by the Zumans and their messy yard. She might have even liked them a little, at one time, and they probably had liked her. Or at least Cissy had. Because why else would Cissy have kept coming over to visit? Had Annie ever thought of that?

Maybe Cissy had looked up to her. Maybe she had just wanted attention.

Maybe she really had cried

And in a moment—as it would again later, after the divorce—Annie's world became not a little brighter, as one might think it should've, but a bit darker. It wasn't necessarily a bad thing. Sometimes, Annie thought—depending upon how you looked at it—it was a beginning.

They were on the edge of a mountain, the car's tires crunching slowly on the wrong side of the winding gravel road.

It's safer here, the wife insisted, both hands sweating on the steering wheel. She could feel it, just a few feet away—the unguarded drop that fell thousands of feet onto large, jagged, body-breaking rocks. But there was also the dazzling mountain-view—a gorgeous, endless, deep-blue, summer morning sky and the handsome, granite faces of the Sierra Nevada. She was missing it all, but she dared not look.

The husband said, I can drive. Do you want to pull over somewhere?

It's okay, she said. Only a few more miles.

With thick patience, the husband did not remind his wife that it was her idea to drive up to this godforsaken town in the first place—this pile of rubble in the middle of nowhere. With no cell service or houses or people. Not even the sound of the wind or birds. Just silence, barrenness, the too-bright sunshine. He did not remind her. But she could feel it, and she could see it—the heavy disapproval and the weary, familiar lines etching themselves across his face.

In Bodie, the wife took pictures of lonely log cabins with tattered curtains in the windows, deserted stores and shuttered businesses, a bank with only two walls and a vault left standing. The husband kicked small rocks around in the dirt and sat in whatever shade he could find. Together they watched a film about Bodie's ten mines, the sixty-five saloons, the numerous red-light houses, the famines and snowstorms during which many of its residents had perished, the wild drinking and shootings that killed the others, and the Bad Man of Bodie, who might have been a real person named Tom Adams, or another man, named Washoe Pete. The Bad Man had shot a saloonkeeper for not serving his drink fast enough. He had murdered a Frenchman for cheating at a game of cards, and an Irishman for offending him one fine Sunday.

At the gift shop, the wife bought a mug with a picture of the Bad Man, skinny and handsome, wearing full cowboy regalia, and a straggly, mean-looking mustache. While she was mulling over a display of fake gold coins by the door, her husband bought an antique knife.

The husband was in a good mood over his unexpected find, and so didn't mind clowning around a bit with his wife before they left Bodie. After all, they would be on their way to Tahoe soon. He pretended to swipe at his wife a few times with the rusty knife. Then the clerk securely wrapped up the knife in white-tissue paper and put it in a plastic bag.

Look, said the wife, pointing to a crumbling shack with a barred door near the store. That used to be the jail.

The husband-turned-clown swaggered into the shack and shut the door, making faces at his wife behind the bars. She smiled, took the camera out of her bag, and shot several photos. The husband rattled the bars.

On their way back down the mountain, the husband drove and together they admired the evening sky, red from the setting sun, and the magnificent mountain scenery. The mug and antique knife lay side by side on the back seat, both wrapped in white tissue paper.

P A R A D O X

Four years, to the day, after her husband, Jim, had left her, Abby drove home from work to see a strange creature sitting in her circular driveway, a large dog with three heads and a long, spiky tail. Its black eyes became immense and glittering when it spotted her, and a harsh, low-pitched growl emanated from behind a set of very large, sharp teeth. Abby backed the sedan away, and drove quickly to her friends' house, twin sisters named Taylor and Tessa; they lived nearest by, and both had once also been friends with Jim.

Taylor and Tessa lived on the other side of town, a hilly neighborhood, near the mountains. Quiet, shadowed streets fell steeply away here, into the darkness of the surrounding forests; it always seemed hushed and still. Even when children ran up and down the streets or shouted at each other from their bikes (the streets were empty of children now), their noises were muffled and absorbed by the huge, silent trees.

Taylor and Tessa lived in a tall, white-clapboard house. When Taylor opened the door, dressed elegantly in white pants, a sleeveless, green shirt, a filmy, pink scarf knotted around her neck, Abby could see the usual myriad of long, winding hallways, snaking away into separate darknesses, behind her friend's shoulder.

There's a creature in my driveway, Abby began, trying to describe the thing, and Taylor gave a small start, nervously smoothing down her already perfect brown hair. We'll call the police, of course, Taylor said, don't worry, you can stay with us. She murmured something over the hallway phone, and then Abby followed her to the back parlor, where Taylor said she and her sister were having lunch.

It seemed as if they were forever going down one hall, and then another, and then another. Abby couldn't remember the house being so large—she also didn't recognize this portion of the house. The halls were not exactly dark here but washed in a kind of tea-colored half-light so peculiar to old houses with many rooms and narrow hallways.

In the back parlor, Tessa perched on the edge of a sofa, wearing exactly the same outfit as her sister, and Abby had the strange impression that Taylor had somehow transferred herself over to the sofa without her noticing.

Tessa said, putting down her coffee cup, smeared with pink lipstick, I think it's time we told you. And Abby asked, told me what?

Jim's here, Taylor said. Abby turned to look at her, as the voice had come from her direction, but Taylor's face was still, like a doll's, the eyes like black glass.

The blood rushed up to Abby's face. That's not very funny, she said. For how could Jim--her Jim--be here? Her friends knew very well he had left the state; they, being wealthy, were the ones who had hired the private detective. Tracked him and his young secretary down to a hotel in Vegas.

Tessa giggled. Oh, he's been here all along, she said. But he didn't want you to know, until now. Abby found herself following Taylor again, down endless hallways, with Tessa now walking behind her.

They went down one steep flight of stairs, into a sort of the basement, and Taylor stopped at a white-painted door, which seemed to lead down another flight of stone steps, to a dirt-floored cellar. At the bottom, in a small circle of light, Abby could see something—-a pair of black shoes. They looked like Jim's work Oxfords, but she couldn't be sure.

I want to leave, she said. This is a sick joke.

But the sisters continued to stand there, grinning at her, pointing down the stairs, looking more and more like clones of each other. Since when had they been so identical? Taylor had always been the taller and prettier of the two, but now, their faces looked exactly alike, and there was no difference in their heights. Don't you want to see Jim? They said, he's waiting for you! They burst out laughing, their eyes immense and glittering, and Abby took this opportunity to push them out of the way. A substance like thick, wet paint stuck to her hands. Patches of silver scales gleamed on their arms where she had rubbed off the color. Abby was back up the stairs, now, onto the landing, but where could she go?

All the hallways looked the same.

WEDDING DAY AT ST. THOMAS

On Sophie's wedding day, this last Saturday in June, it is unseasonably cool, and all is unusually still and silent in this small Midwestern town of Rollins, Iowa, firmly embedded, or entombed, as it were, into a surrounding patchwork of idyllic woods, grassy hills, and rolling soy and corn fields. Sophie and her fiancé, Ben, have arrived early together, though she remembers, somewhere, that arriving together isn't good luck. She has tried to do as much as she could according to the rules, but what rules or whose rules, she is—and never really was—quite clear on, and neither can she do everything correctly anyway, even if she had wanted to. She wasn't raised here but is an immigrant from the other side of the world. She had moved here to the Midwest with her family when she was eight—what works on one side of the world may not on the other. What has happened, then, with this wedding Sophie has completely planned herself, is that it has become a conglomeration, a hodge-podge of things she learned from her surroundings, things she learned from her family, things she learned from books, and things she simply wanted to do. It is a unique wedding, she can at least say.

One thing she did not expect is that the weather is not good for a wedding. She and Ben had assumed since they would all be indoors, it wouldn't matter, but now, it seems it does. Black clouds fill the sky and create an all too somber mood for such an occasion. It only increases Sophie's sense of panic and doom, things she knows she shouldn't be feeling, at least not to this overwhelming degree, on this most important of days. But Sophie realizes there isn't any time left to ponder over what to do or how to fix this, whether by taking a painkiller, which she doesn't have on hand anyway, or by fleeing, which she can't bring herself to do, even for a few minutes: people are arriving, men in dark suits and women in pastel cloud-like summer dresses, all disappearing into the depths of St. Thomas's Episcopal Church in noiseless and orderly groups. There are a few children—small girls in puffy-sleeved dresses and restless boys in starched jacket-and-shorts sets—who are also subdued and silent, as they follow their parents inside. The creaking sounds of an organ escape into the chilly air every time the doors are opened.

St. Thomas's is the oldest building in Rollins, built in 1810, a landmark even before the town had formally incorporated. It was intended as a large, sprawling place of worship, a central point for the five or six small farming communities located around its perimeter, but now it sits in the midst of a busy college town, only one of at least forty other churches in Rollins, but still implacable and solid, with its long, broad walls of golden-brown stone and rows of tall, rectangular windows. Next door stands another of the town's oldest buildings—St. Catherine's Catholic Church. St. Catherine's is as tall and straight, as St. Thomas's is stout and rambling; it is built of pale-gray stone and possesses a magnificent, stained-glass rose window, which looks upon the main street like a kaleidoscopic eye. Surrounding these two ancient buildings are row upon row of newer frame houses, converted into student apartments, restaurants, and a variety of small businesses catering to the college community. Across the street, the modern glass and steel buildings of the university architecture and computer science buildings gleam with severe beauty, even on the cloudiest days such as this. There are plenty of historic buildings on campus—the English department is still housed in a red-brick Victorian mansion, for example. On Sunday mornings, fresh-faced college girls and scrubbed-clean boys in their best clothes spill out of the carved oak doors onto the sidewalks and streets, greeting one another, discussing where to go for lunch or what to do that afternoon. But today is not a Sunday, but a Saturday, and the doors of the surrounding churches are closed, as if to the dead, while the black clouds mass steadily overhead. St. Thomas's bustles quietly, and soon after the clock tower on the university campus strikes two, sounds of an organ playing Albinoni's "Adagio" echoes out of the heavy doors, and the last of the people who linger outside hurry in.

St. Thomas's inside is just as crusty and antiquated as its exterior, a place full of candles and velvet hangings and rows of long wooden benches. Even so, this church is spare compared to some of the others Sophie has visited—such as St. Catherine's next door, which is much more lavishly decorated, with an abundance of carvings and marble statues of angels and saints and crimson-streaked Jesuses-on-crosses. Sophie attended a Sunday mass once with a friend and was intrigued and fascinated by the excess. At twenty, Sophie is only vaguely concerned she has no real affiliation herself—she was raised in a Christian family, and then out of curiosity attended Apostolic, Presbyterian, and Baptist services with friends. During these visits, she tried listening attentively to the sermons or lectures, but her interest never lasted long, and her thoughts would wander to anything else besides what was being said; she particularly enjoyed admiring the jewel-like colors of the stained-glass windows, if there happened to be any (and there usually were). Afterwards. she smiled and talked to the other church goers—and the next day, she remembered very little about what had happened or been said. It was as if she had been in a dream. Besides, there were classes to attend, schoolwork to do, a job in the evenings, Ben to spend time with. Now Sophie attends St. Thomas's only because Ben attends St. Thomas's, and because his family has always attended Episcopalian churches. And here they are, because it is where people go when they get married. *I am getting married*, Sophie tells herself again, for the hundredth time, and still the words do not connect, they are words in a novel or in a movie, describing somebody else.

"A little closer!" the photographer calls out. Sophie inches closer to Ben who is grinning and sweating in his black wool suit and starched white shirt.

Sophie whispers to him, "This is taking longer than I thought." To which Ben does not reply, but only continues to grin. Perhaps he does not hear her. They have already spent an hour taking pictures with Anne, Sophie's best friend and maid of honor, and Daniel, Ben's friend and best man. Anne and Daniel have been relegated to the back pews now, waiting for the service to start.

The guests wander, as if lost souls, around the church, the organ plays on, the photographer snaps away, and Sophie can only identify emotions closer to terror than excitement or joy. She wants to scream in frustration. She wants it all to be over. Sections of her dress, a snowy-white chiffon that comes down to just below her knees, stick to Ben's suit like leaves of damp tissue paper. Sophie did not spend much time picking out her dress. She only knew she wanted something different, not the usual long gown, and so she had gone to the mall and picked this out; she realizes now with some dismay, that the dress is probably more suitable for a summer cocktail party than a wedding dress. But isn't that all right for a small informal wedding such as this? Why hadn't her mother helped her choose something?

Her mother had not helped plan any part of the wedding. Whether this was out of respect for her daughter's ideas or out of disinterest, Sophie does not know. Still, it is a pretty dress, Sophie reassures herself, and tries to smile brightly when the photographer calls out once more. The guests in the front pews—Ben's family and aunts and uncles—gaze at the wedding couple on the altar and whisper to each other as if they are exhibitions at a circus or museum. There is his tiny, bird-like mother in a new lemon-colored suit, his father, with his usual inscrutable expression and bent-backed slouch, and two uncles and an aunt from New York Sophie has never seen before. They smile and nod good-naturedly at the self-conscious couple. Sophie's own parents sit in the front row on the opposite side, her mother in a pink suit and wearing the same stretchy smile she always wears in public, and her stocky, jovial father in a light gray suit. They talk only to Sophie's older brother, Michael, sitting next to them.

"This is the last one," the photographer apologizes and clicks his camera again. "Perfect!" The sky outside darkens to a night-time blackness, and raindrops begin to sprinkle against the long rows of windows.

Someone says, "it's raining." But Sophie does not mind but rather welcomes the sight of the winding streams of water upon the window

Ben loosens the tie around his neck, and says, in his usual calm manner, "It doesn't matter. Everyone is here. We can start now."

The organ begins to play Mussorgsky's "Pictures at an Exhibition," a signal the processional is about to start. Everyone shuffles into place and the small wedding party begins down the aisle. Sophie walks slowly towards the minister, towards Ben, in a daze, her father by her side, clutching her gardenia bouquet; she cannot believe all these people seated in the pews are here for her and Ben, to watch them get married. Never before has she been the focus of anything. She reaches the altar in perfect timing with the end of the organ piece. Ben stands there, flushed and young-looking. Everybody always comments on what a smart and nice person Ben is, how incredibly successful he will be. He is the kind of person who helps out anybody who needs it, at the cost even, of his own comfort and time. Somehow, however, his "niceness" has never impressed Sophie, as much as it probably should. Ben is considered the smartest of his circle of already brilliant friends, and that is what she admires most about him. He is good to her, and generous—surely, he is the perfect person to marry. But when Sophie looks at him, she does not feel love or even affection, only a confused kind of wonder, even alarm—was she really marrying this man? For the past few weeks they had discussed with the minister "what they were getting into" and they had nodded impatiently and agreed to everything he said, but now…did they really know? She has been Ben's girlfriend for two years; she feels towards him, standing there now, what she would towards a nice relative, or one of her friends. There were never any violent passions—things had always been ordinary, steady, and comfortable. A haze settles upon Sophie's thoughts, like damp wads of cotton, and she only wants to have this all done with, she doesn't want to think about this anymore. She will perform her part, say all the right things at the right time, smile or remain solemn at the correct intervals. She feels as if this day, this whole ceremony dragging on interminably, is all unreal, as if she were in a silent movie. Though she can see the minister's lips moving, she cannot hear or understand what he is saying; the words are just noises that drift in and out of her consciousness. She only speaks when certain parts of the drifting noises trigger a response from somewhere in her memory. The echoing bang of the organ awakens her finally, and she moves slowly back down the aisle, a newly married woman. A numbness has spread over her entire body, has frozen her brain. But through all that coldness, something speaks, in a voice so quiet that Sophie only feels it as the slightest pinprick: "This isn't how it's supposed to be."

The reception is held at the Coach House Restaurant, where they have reserved a private dining room. One long table, covered with an immaculate white cloth, stands at the back of the room, and several round tables, equally dressed, are arranged on either side of it. In the middle of the restaurant is the wedding cake, perched on a round table of its own. The cake is a smallish, two-tiered, white-sponge affair, with smooth walls of ivory fondant icing, five red sugar roses around the base, and three on top. There are no other ornaments. Sophie, spotting the plain, lonely cake, wonders why she had chosen such a simple design—at the time, it had seemed elegant and unfussy, but now, it was just boring. But like her dress, there is nothing to be done about it now. Besides, people do not notice and do not care. They are more interested in dinner—many people have already seated themselves at the tables (including many Sophie does not recognize) while still more stream into the room. Sophie floats from table to table, greeting people she has not seen in years. Her parents talk to her only briefly before going off and socializing with Ben's parents and their friends.

"Sophie!" calls a familiar-looking woman with short, fair hair. It is Susan, a favorite classmate from grade school.

"I'm so glad to see you," smiles Sophie, taking hold of her friend's hands. "Thank you so much for coming." This is probably the happiest she has felt all day. Susan's appearance is such a pleasant surprise, in contrast to the varying levels of anxiety, fear and stress she has felt all day. She would prefer to be with Susan and her other childhood friends outside, walking barefoot in a creek in the woods, on a sunny summer day, as they used to when they were all young.

"Well, of course I had to come!" says Susan, looking not at all like the tall, disheveled girl with freckles Sophie last remembers. Now, Susan is wearing a flowered dress, still tall and sturdy, but with neat bobbed hair and makeup. "Look at you! All married now!" Susan is in medical school, Sophie knows. She has kept up on the whereabouts of her classmates through Jamie, who seems to know everybody or at least, knew someone else who knew what everyone was doing. There are the usual number of housewives and teachers and office workers and hair stylists. Sophie labels herself a "student" even though she is attending class only part-time. She works at the library during the evenings and weekends, a job she tolerates to pay the bills and tuition. Ben is also in graduate school, already working on his master's in engineering. They always planned to get married as soon as Sophie finished her freshman year. They had wanted a small wedding, but now, the number of guests seem rather sizable. The faces begin to blur as Sophie nods and smiles and talks with table after table of relatives and friends, mostly Ben's friends, she realizes. The dinner is excellent—prime rib, salad, mashed potatoes, green beans—and afterwards, Sophie and Ben walk together around the room, toasting each table. When they reach Daniel's table, where he sits sweating, plump and raucous, with five other of Ben's good friends, Sophie feels her guardedness spring up. This is a man not known for his tact or good manners. Sure enough, Daniel shouts out, "A kiss! A kiss!" after the toast, and Sophie freezes in embarrassment. The last thing she wants now is to kiss Ben, especially in front of everybody. She has always hated this kind of thing. After a few more insistent shouts from Daniel, Ben awkwardly bends over and kisses her on the cheek. And though, of course, she and Ben have kissed a countless number of times, engaged in much more intimate things than this, this first kiss given to her by her husband, after they were officially wed, is one of the most terrible moments in her life.

The week goes on as it always has—there is no honeymoon. They continue on with the normal rhythm of their lives the day after their wedding, as if nothing had happened. Perhaps this is to be expected. Marriage is a mere formality after living together for two years.

"We'll go to Paris someday," Sophie suggests, "when we have more money." Ben thinks this is sensible. Besides, he has an important deadline coming up—a journal article due in two months. It isn't the first time Sophie wishes he wasn't so practical—she would have much preferred a surprise getaway, even if it had only been a few days at a local hotel or bed and breakfast. But Ben is not the type to plan getaways. Of any type. Sophie has the feeling, which she hopes is wrong, that he looks down upon such things, rather than being merely ignorant of them.

Ben attends his classes in the mornings and teaches in the afternoon. Sophie straightens the apartment, runs errands in the morning, and works at the dusty Physical

Sciences Reading Room in the afternoons. Usually she and Ben meet for lunch at one of the cafes on campus.

After lunch, Sophie always takes a walk around the lake. One thing Sophie refuses to do is to walk around town. She doesn't like walking near houses and people and traffic. All those cars and people and staring—not just the people, for houses can stare, too—bothers her. She feels—she knows—that no matter how long she is has lived in this area, she will never fit in. But she does want to be outside, with the trees, grass, and sunshine—just as long as it is as far away from others as possible. She even finds it hard to tolerate the others she encounters on the gravel walking paths around the lake—should she say hello, ignore them, look at them, not look at them, and so forth— and she is afraid of the bicyclists who ride as fast as possible, round and round the lake. She feels like they might knock her over.

The first day after their wedding she takes her walk on a Tuesday. She thinks she should feel different, being married, but she doesn't, not at all. Earlier, she had looked at herself in the mirror, and she is the same as she has always been. Her height and small features often lead others to believe she is much younger than she really is. This mistake annoys her, although she tries to remember she will be grateful for her youthful appearance later. Her black eyes have a strange, unsettling look. When angry, her eyes can become frightening. *Cut your eyes out*, her mother would hiss to her as a child. She was not allowed to talk back, so remained silent, but her eyes must have shown what she felt. Maybe this was why her mother seemed afraid of her, why she disliked Sophie so much, why she punished her constantly. Wasn't that why she said those things? *You will never find anyone to marry you. So ugly and fat. Look at those legs. Why are you wearing those pants? They're too tight. Go change.* Her mother never screamed. She said it quietly, with that scraping, hissing tone.

When Ben first met her mother, he told Sophie her mother was nice, and she did look sweet and quiet, in her prim pale-pink suit, the carefully bobbed hair, glasses, and subdued make-up. Her mother always spoke softly in public and smiled often, sometimes giggled like a little girl. Sophie feels big and thick and bumbling next to her mother, although Sophie is actually shorter and smaller. *Would you like some cake*, Ben had asked Sophie's mother deferentially at the reception, offering her a plate. It is only right, after all, that one be polite to one's mother-in-law. People can change, can't they? It is hard to believe this gentle, middle-aged woman was the same monster Sophie had described. Maybe she hadn't been all that bad. Sophie sometimes exaggerates, Ben has said, she is too sensitive. Sophie herself always assumes a mild and neutral expression when speaking to her mother. They aren't warm and loving, like maybe daughters and mothers should be, but they aren't hateful towards each other, either. What Sophie feels around her mother during her wedding, what she feels when she observes not only Ben's, but the entire room of guests' deference to her parents she still does not know, she cannot identify. It is something puzzling, maybe it is just nothing. Emptiness.

Sophie works in both the Main Library and across the street in the Physical Sciences Reading Room, in the Chemistry Building. The Chemistry Building is one of the older structures on campus, a sprawling, brick, Gothic house with dark, tiled hallways, and tall, mullioned windows. The dim hallways seem empty most of the time, even during school hours, when students walk to and from classes and lecture halls. It is as if the students are merely ghosts—passing noise and shadows along the walls and floors—disappearing as quickly and quietly as the late afternoon sunshine on the tiles. Sophie does not feel scared working in the Reading Room, going to and from work, but there is sometimes a frisson, a shiver of nervousness, a feeling that the very building itself is watching her, listening to her footsteps. She is glad the Reading Room closes no later than seven in the evenings.

Her supervisor is a tall, thin lady in her mid-thirties. Miss Osborne wears glasses and wears her long oak-colored hair in a messy bun at the back of her head. She speaks softly, rapidly, her topaz-colored eyes staring without blinking. She rarely smiles. Sophie is a little afraid of Miss Osborne, as she is a little afraid of all her employers, although Miss Osborne never gives her cause for any fear.

She is not friendly, but neither is she harsh. Sophie shrinks from Miss Osborne instinctively—her frail look, her quiet, manner reminds her of other women she knows who look like this, such as her mother

Miss Osborne doesn't try to draw Sophie out, but her eyes are kind when she asks how she is doing, or if she wants less hours during or more during vacation. The pay is low, so Sophie always wants more hours, finals or not. She is often at the Reading Room ten hours a week and at the Main Library for fifteen. She is thankful for Ben's graduate pay, and his parents send him money every holiday. They are not wealthy—and probably make far less than her own parents—yet they give Ben whatever they can. Her parents have not sent her anything in the past two years. After work, she often meets with Ben, and they would splurge on dinner at one of the cheap Chinese restaurants on campus. One place in particular, run by a middle-aged Chinese couple, charges only three dollars for a plate piled high with food. They eat here quite frequently. Although it seems a humdrum life, it is all Sophie and Ben have ever known, while they have been together.

It is at this restaurant Sophie is meeting Ben tonight. It is another hot summer evening with gloomy gray skies. As she sits down to sip her tea and wait for Ben—who is always late—a sharp pain pierces through her side and abdomen. She feels nauseous and light-headed. *I just need something to eat,* she tells herself. Ben shows up after her food has already arrived and she starts on her second helping of chicken and mushrooms.

"Sorry, I was starving," she says—it's counter service here, where customers order first and then find seats. She could've waited for Ben, she supposes, but rationalizes one dish wasn't enough for her today, anyway.

"No problem," Ben says, in his usual easygoing way. "Sorry I'm late. I'm really behind on my paper. What did you order?"

"Chicken with mushrooms. What about you?"

"Beef with broccoli. Do we have plans for tonight? I might go back to the lab after dinner."

"No, it's fine," Sophie waits for a moment, and then says. "I haven't been feeling well lately. Nauseated and tired. I'm feeling better now, after eating, but...perhaps..."

They both look at each other and need to say no more.

"Do you really think..."

"Maybe. I'll pick up the test kit tonight."

They eat in silence, and then speak on other subjects— Ben's work, Sophie 's work, how classes were going. Ben is considering job prospects after graduation, which is now less than a year away. They sometimes speak of moving to California or some other state, far away from the Midwest. Sophie mentions quitting her library jobs again and finding something that pays more.

"But what would you do?"

"There's restaurant work. Maybe I could get better job experience, with a real company. These university jobs just pay so little, and they're so very boring."

Ben doesn't seem swayed one way or another, so Sophie resolves once again to look in the help wanted sections in the newspaper.

Ben walks to the lab after dinner, and Sophie walks home alone in the fading twilight. She doesn't enjoy being on the busy campus streets, although she loves the sunset hours. She dreams of being somewhere leafy and quiet and green, and almost enjoys the solitary stroll back, in her other world, although cars rush past, sometimes with music blaring from the windows.

They live in one of the many frame house-turned-apartment buildings around the university. Theirs is a unit on the third floor, a cozy and bright attic space, outfitted with old mismatched appliances, threadbare carpet, an ancient bathroom, and many small nooks and crannies. The odd spaces and unusual design of the apartment are part of the charm of the place—the dark hallway, for example, connecting the living room to the rest of the apartment is a long L-shape, with one small, square window and a built-in shelf below. Sophie had applied an adhesive-backed, stained-glass window covering to the window, so that the light filters in with muted colors.

The kitchen is the largest room in the house, long and narrow, with yellow linoleum and one tall window at the end, and the bathroom has a tub placed right below a low, sloping ceiling. No stand-up shower is possible. Sophie loves the apartment for all its sunshine and quirks and there is no place she would rather be, at the moment. It is her and Ben's home, their very own little place, a beautiful, little nest. She could spend her entire life here, just like this, she really believes. Just the two of them.

It is ten-thirty and Ben is still at the lab. Sophie has already picked up the test kit. Of course, it is positive. She is excited at first, and calls Ben to let him know. Ben sounds excited, too. *I'll be home as soon as I can,* he reassures her. But as Sophie sits waiting, attempting to do her homework that night, she somehow feels less and less happy. She feels ill and tired, and there are still five problems left to finish before nine tomorrow morning. Tomorrow is also her long day at work—she would have to go straight to the library after her classes and stay there until close. The equations on the page look strange and incomprehensible, like some kind of alien hieroglyphics. *I can do it*, she tells herself. *Just concentrate.* A few years ago, she had taken an aptitude test which had shown she had almost equal math and verbal abilities. Yet, she has always hated math—looking at math problems frightens her. It has been like this since she was in elementary school. She remembers sitting in the basement of her home, crying over high school math workbooks, rubbing the eraser over and over on the page until it creates a hole in the grainy paper. She was not allowed to come upstairs until the page of problems were finished. She can't remember if she ever did finish those problems, but obviously her mother let her come upstairs at some point.

She feels herself absent-mindedly rubbing her eraser on the lined graph paper, until the page is empty again. Then, she begins sketching a face on the page—a girl's face with long dark hair and dark eyes. She uses the little squares on the page to make sure both eyes are exactly the same size and shape.

There is a scraping at the door, and Ben appears, exhausted and slightly disheveled; he smiles when he catches sight of her. "Still up?" he says. "Sorry it took so long. But I have some good news." He gives her a hug, and she prepares two mugs of tea.

"Homework due tomorrow," she says. "Are you hungry? I could heat up a pizza."

"No, this is fine. How are you feeling?"

"Not that great."

"You'll have to take better care of yourself," Ben says, and she believes he really is happy. Ben shows positive feelings less than negative, and she knows him well enough to see he is pleased. But this makes her shrink inside herself even more.

"Ben," she says. "Don't you think we're too young right now. I still have school."

"People have been having kids at our age for a long time. I don't think so. We'll be fine."

"But we don't have to have kids. Not right now at least."

Ben looks at her with concern—or was it alarm? "What are you saying?" he asks.

"Just that, I may not be ready for a child. You knew how I grew up, and I probably won't be good with kids."

Ben takes the cup from her hands and gives her a hug. "I know you'll be great," he says. "Don't worry. Maybe we can talk about this later. I have some news to share with you that might help."

"Yes, that's right," she says, feeling embarrassed for not having remembered, and tries to smile. "What is it?"

He says his thesis advisor has been recommending him for a research job on the West Coast, with a company that produces scientific instruments.

"Remember that interview from the spring?" Sophie nods and tries to smile. "There is a position opening up next year, and they want me to start as soon as I graduate." He beams proudly. Sophie smiles, as she really is happy about the job. And they would be moving to California!

"But what about school? And the baby?"

For the first time that evening, Ben's face falls, as if he had just been confronted with something bothersome and slightly unpleasant. "We'll be here when the baby is born. And then you could also transfer to a school out West."

"That's true," Sophie says, feeling a little more positive. Going to a school out in California sounds exciting.

"Okay," she says, although she resolves to stop by Planned Parenthood the next day to pick up some information. They have an office nearby, which she and Ben often passes while walking to classes. *It won't hurt just to get some information after all,* she told herself. Ben didn't need to know about it.

Usually she is so happy about the baby, she just tells herself over and over again, "I am going to be a mom. I am going to be a mom!" After work or classes, she stops by and looks at all the baby clothes in the campus town's only consignment shop. She touches all the soft, tiny pajamas, and smiles at all the little hats and adorable T-shirts, decorated with ducks or sheep or stars. She carefully sorts through all the toys, and finds a shiny silver rattle—she bought it for only a dollar. Another time she bought an almost-new pajama set in daffodil-yellow for five dollars, and another time she buys a crisp, white lace baby dress with pearl buttons, lovingly nestled in a satin-pillowed box. The angelic dress costs more—twelve dollars. She does not know if the baby is going to be a girl or boy yet, but she likes the dress and wants to look at it. I can always give it as a present to someone else, she tells herself. But she knows she never would. She will always keep it, even if she never has a baby girl.

Ben is increasingly excited about the baby—he is proud to be a dad, Sophie can tell. He fusses over her and makes sure she gets as much rest as possible and he tries to be home earlier from the lab. He cooks her steaks and gets her ice cream and pickles. You have to eat well, he says, and Sophie thinks, wow, I can live with this. She has never been so spoiled before. She does often feel ill, but her appetite thankfully does not disappear as she thought it would.

Then there are the dark days. Days when she can't get up because she is too tired, but still has classes or work. Days when looking at baby clothes depresses her, because she is by herself and there is no one else to talk to about the baby. She and Ben have decided not to tell anyone yet.

"Maybe in a month or two," he reassures her.

"Do you think they'll be happy about it?" Sophie asks. She feels the reaction will not be good. "They're going to think we're too young."

"No, no, don't think like that," Ben says. "Of course, they'll be happy."

Sophie remains gloomy. But aren't she and Ben following the path their own parents had taken so many years ago? Yes, her mother was older when she had Sophie, but essentially, isn't this what they are supposed to do? Sophie had asked her mother years ago why she had had children, and her mother had replied quite simply, "That's what everyone else did. That's what everyone does—have children and families."

"And you quit your doctoral degree to raise us? Didn't you want to finish it?"

"No," her mother said. "It was more important to raise you children. That's what Dad and I agreed on."

"Do you wish you had stayed and gotten your degree?" Sophie persisted.

"No," said her mother, without hesitation. "I didn't want to."

Sophie didn't believe this. First of all, her mother had hated almost all aspects of being a parent. She didn't like cooking, she had never read to Sophie or spent time playing with her as a young child, she rarely did housekeeping—Sophie was given this responsibility as she became older—and she did not in any way resemble those nice mothers Sophie read about in her story books or saw on television. Instead, Sophie remembers her mother mostly sitting at the dining room table, doing paperwork, or working on bills, going back and forth from her father's office, and then, during her free time, playing golf with her father or shopping. Sophie remembers many boring trips to the department store waiting while her mother tries on outfit after outfit—she sometimes asks Sophie for her opinion, and Sophie usually dutifully smiles and nods. She had been bored to the point of numbness during these excursions.

These are things she does not want to dwell on, but it seems being alone so much, it is unavoidable. One sunny day, when the weather is starting to turn and the leaves are no longer bright but falling off in brown papery masses, she stops by the Planned Parenthood office. She picks up a brochure and flees. Once home, she pores over the materials and reads everything carefully. She is still in her early stages, and it would be no problem to do the procedure. Of course, there is the cost—three hundred dollars. She could put it on her credit card. She tries to bring it up with the campus doctor—the woman is nice, but definitely not helpful. *Of course, that is completely your decision*, the doctor says, but her voice is neutral to the point of being disapproving. Sophie calls the Planned Parenthood office, and they are friendly and helpful and say they can set up an appointment, no problem. Sophie tells them she will call back.

She knows her old childhood friends will not understand—they would be shocked. And anyway, she has only one fairly close friend—Elizabeth—she could even possibly talk it over with; but she can almost see Elizabeth's disapproving and uncomfortable face now. They had never talked about anything that deeply personal. Sophie has another friend, Rosie—an old college roommate, who is deeply religious. She loves Rosie, but Rosie—who is very strong-willed and outspoken—certainly would never agree.

She mentions it to Ben, of course; at first, he is willing to listen and seems open to the idea, but he grows increasingly against it. It's wrong, he says simply, but he doesn't entirely say *no* either. *You can if that's what you want,* he says and turns away. *I am not going to agree with it, though.* Fair enough, Sophie thinks to herself. He wants to have the baby and I'm the one who is ambivalent. She tries to be happy again, tries to forget the dark thoughts.

Sophie makes the appointment, for a Friday morning. She cancels work for that day, making up some reason about going out of town.

She does not tell Ben about the appointment. He is so excited about the baby, so sure everything is going to be perfect. She can't bring herself to tell him. She spends most of her time, running through in her panicked brain all the ways she can bring up the subject; she tries to think of all the possibilities. She finds it very hard to think.

She is still able to do all of her work well, but often catches herself staring at her desk, feeling nothing in particular, just staring, her mind blank. She is beginning to feel cold, sick, and nervous all the time now, instead of just occasionally—she scarcely notices the lovely August weather, so warm and gently sunny. School will be starting soon again. Sometimes when she cannot stand it anymore, she calls the Planned Parenthood office just to chat with someone and go over the details and her options again.

Two days before her scheduled abortion, she calls and cancels, blaming the money situation. She doesn't have three hundred dollars and she doesn't want to put this on her credit card. But the real reason she cancels is because there is no one who will or can go to the appointment with her. She feels resigned to fate and is angry at herself for being so weak and lacking in independence. But at least she won't be stuck in this small town forever—she and Ben will be moving to the sunny and beautiful West Coast, and she can continue school out there. She will be a mom and do the best she can. That's all she feels capable of hoping for, at this point.

The first babysitter arrived at ten in the morning. Heidi Thomas. She was young, tanned, plump, and pretty. She wore shiny black polish on her very long fingernails, and beetle-black lipstick. We sat on our one sofa, Heidi and I, and Mike, my short, round, and compact two-year-old son, sat between us.

"So, Heidi," I said, getting right down to business. "Why do you want to be a babysitter?"

"Oh, I just love children," said Heidi.

Mike tugged at my sleeve and demanded juice. I told him I would get it later.

"You work in the mornings now, is that right? So, you can come in from noon until five."

Heidi nodded. She tried to smile at Mike, too, but he would have none of it.

"Mommy," he said. "I'm thirsty."

"I'm talking to Heidi right now," I told him. "I'll get it later."

Then he said, loudly and clearly, "Dumb babysitter!" Heidi's smile froze on her face.

"Mike!" I said sternly. "That's not nice!" He grinned, jumped off the sofa, and scurried off to his bedroom.

"I'm so sorry," I told Heidi. "I think he's tired."

"Oh, that's okay," said Heidi, with the same frozen grin. "He's cute."

I was beginning to feel a little skeptical about Heidi but seized this opportunity to test her. "Mike says things like that sometimes. Sometimes, he also throws things when he's upset. How would you handle that if you were watching him?"

Heidi seemed at a loss for an answer, but finally replied, "I would tell him to stop."

I waited for her to expand, nodded, and smiled encouragingly, but Heidi was done. This was a disappointment because I had wanted to like Heidi, thought it might even work out—but probably, I knew she was wrong from the moment I laid eyes on the long, sharp, pointy fingernails. And she was growing more wrong by the minute.

Mike bounced back into the room, brandishing his play sword. "Yah!" he shouted, pointing the sword at Heidi. She sat and valiantly tried to keep smiling.

"Heidi's rude!" Mike screeched.

"Mike!" I said, as firmly as I could. "Please go to your room until I'm done talking to Heidi."

"I don't like Heidi!" Mike called from the hallway.

"I'm so sorry about that," I said to Heidi. "I don't know what's wrong with him today."

"Oh, that's okay," she said again, though by now the smile had slid from her face, and she sat, staring after Mike as if he were some large insect.

"Thank you for coming," I said. "I'll let you know by tomorrow. Did you have any questions?"

"Uh, I don't think so," she said. "How much did you say you were paying again?"

My answer apparently reminded Heidi of why she had come in the first place, for she brightened up, and said in a chirpy voice, "Oh, okay! You can call me on my cell phone! Any time! You know, if you can't reach me at home."

"Mike," I said to my son, after she had departed. "I'm glad you told me how you felt about Heidi, but next time you should tell me after she goes home."

He looked up at me with his big, brown, mischievous eyes and smiled his gummy smile, and I couldn't help but shake my head and smile back at him.

After Heidi, there was Florence. Over the phone, I found out Florence was older and from New Jersey. She sounded intelligent and funny, and I was eager to meet her. For example, when I asked, what would she do if Mike called her stupid, she said, "Well, I would say, 'I don't think I'm stupid.'"

Florence, in other words, amused me—and I was not often amused by the applicants we received. Infuriated or dismayed, yes, but rarely amused.

"I think she may be the one," I informed my husband, Larry, the day Florence was due at our house for her first in-person interview.

"I should never have advertised the salary," I continued. "Most of the callers are terrible. I can hear the desperation in their voices."

I had thought that by offering a higher wage, the ad might extract higher quality applicants, but in fact, it seemed to have achieved the opposite effect—those who called usually asked first about the money, or the hours, but never about the children. Most had very bad manners. Very few could even speak in coherent sentences.

"Are you sure we should do this? Maybe Mike's still too young."

"No, I'm not sure," I said. "But how can I work if I have to watch him all day."

I was considering taking a reporting job, based in D.C. I would be able to work at home some of the time, but I still needed someone to watch over Mike.

"You don't have to take that job," said Larry.

I lowered my voice, "I think he's ready for a babysitter. And *I'm* ready for a babysitter—I've been very impatient with him lately. I yelled at him yesterday just for knocking over a cup of milk."

Thinking about yesterday's incident again made me cringe. I knew, of course, it had been an accident, that Mike had not knocked over the glass to annoy me, and yet I had still gotten unreasonably angry, especially since it had happened after a long day of time-consuming, energy-sapping, mind-numbing errands. It was nearing the end of October, and thus the beginning of the holiday season—Halloween was less than a week away. And so, we had shopped for a costume for Mike (and found nothing he liked), shopped for Halloween decorations, shopped for groceries, dragged ourselves to the post office, bank, and library, and gotten Mike a much-needed haircut.

"This'll be a big change for him," said Larry. I nodded but did not reply. We had gone over the same conversation a hundred times before, and I had gone over it on my own another thousand times. How could I possibly leave my beloved Mike with someone else? I missed him already, thinking of him spending part of his day away from me. "Let's just try it," I said. "If it doesn't work out, we'll just have to think of something else. But a babysitter, someone Mike can get to know well, would be the best way to go."

Someone knocked on the door.

A tall, elderly, balding woman crept in. She smelled strongly of cigarette smoke, and had very bright black eyes and sparse, wet, copper-colored hair, which she combed carefully, with a small black, plastic comb, as soon as she sat down. This was Florence? This was the chatty, clever woman, whom I had befriended on the phone yesterday?

"So nice to finally meet you," I said, trying to smile. "How are you?"

"Fine, thank you," said Florence in a slow, gravelly voice. "And this must be Mike." She leered at him, and he hurried, as fast as he could, behind my chair. I started with my standard interview questions but what really went through my mind were these wonderings: Why hadn't she dried her hair before she arrived? What had she been doing—swimming, taking a shower? And why did she start combing her hair in front of us as though we weren't even there? Was she ill or mentally unstable? It certainly seemed that way. I felt it mostly from her eyes, which had a wild, glassy, overly bright stare, as if she hadn't slept for days or was on some kind of amphetamine. She also carried what looked like a large, plastic, freezer storage bag, crammed with small toys and candy.

"May I give your son a present?" she asked hoarsely.

I nodded politely, although I wanted to say no. Mike's curiosity overcame his fear, and he crept out from behind my chair, and accepted the lollipop Florence held out to him. But then, when she started taking out finger puppets and assembling them for what was apparently an impromptu show, I stood up.

"Thank you, Florence," I said. "But we have to go out soon."

I locked the door after she left, drew the deadbolt, and threw away the lollipop Mike still clutched in his hand, promising to buy him another one.

Larry came in from the other room. He always sat in during the first few minutes of the interview, but then he would leave—he had seen the person and that was all he wanted. He left all the interrogating up to me. I was the former reporter, after all.

"I liked her, Mommy," Mike said, snuggling up against my side. I looked at Larry.

"She was worse than Heidi," was all he said. I resolved never to have Mike around again, while we interviewed. One of us would have to watch him. I didn't want Mike to like anybody until we approved of them.

The phone rang. I went to answer it and it was another call for the ad.

"Where do you live?" I asked, for I saw a Maryland number listed on the caller ID. In my ad, I had specified I only wanted someone from the Fairfax, Virginia area, where we lived.

"Oh, just across the Wilson bridge, near the border," waffled the caller. This was at least twenty miles away. When I hesitated, she spoke patronizingly, "Now don't get frightened."

"I'm not frightened," I said. "And I'm not interested." I slammed the phone down. It rang again. It was The Wilson Bridge caller.

"Could you just listen to me," the woman said.

I said, in my Bartleby-voice, "I prefer not to."

I hung up again and turned off the phone.

After interviewing about ten more prospects, we decided to try preschool. Mike was still too young to go to the Montessori schools I liked, but I chose to investigate some other places, the ones with the biggest ads in the local parenting magazines.

The first preschool Mike and I visited, Forest Lane Children's Academy and Day Care, was located not far from where we lived. We made an appointment to visit on Monday, during the lunch hour.

Forest Lane was a charming, sprawling, two-story, gray stone building, reminiscent of a fairy-tale cottage in the woods. Inside, the school was spotless. There was not a single toy, coat, or cot out of place. This impressed me a great deal. I wondered how they were able to keep the school so clean and organized, with so many children around—and then I saw the school's director, Mrs. Harden, and understood. Mrs. Harden was a very tall, very blond, very neatly groomed woman, with a cropped, military-style haircut. I approved of the woman's regal bearing, her ruthless efficiency, her no-nonsense haircut—all a welcome change from the wild fashions and indolence and lack of maturity and plain strangeness that I had encountered during our nanny-interviewing phase. Here, in this savvy director of Forest Lane Academy, was someone who took charge, who knew what she was doing, who could be trusted not to falter in case of an emergency. Mrs. Harden wasted not a single word while reeling off the school's policies. She firmly reassured me that I "could drop in at any time." Then she offered, in a clipped voice, to take us on a tour of the building. The first place we visited was the kitchen.

"This is Mrs. Orne," Mrs. Harden said, nodding to a grandmotherly lady in an apron that nearly covered her entire pear-shaped body.

"Everything is so clean!" I couldn't help exclaiming. It was nearing the lunch hour and steaming pans of spaghetti lay out on the long tables. The grandmotherly lady—Mrs. Orne—stood stirring the hot sauce and noodles. She smiled at Mike, and called out to him in an easy, friendly manner, "Hello there, young man!"

"Hi!" shouted back Mike. He was very excited to be at the school, in a place so different from our own house, and kept pulling at my hand to see everything he could, as fast as possible.

"What a nice lady," I murmured. Preschool children ran about the kitchen, helping Mrs. Orne set the tables. Indeed, this was a fairy-tale place, and I could see Mike playing happily here.

We stopped by the gym, which was then serving as the nap room for the smaller children. Though the room was filled with children on cots (none of them sleeping, I noticed), it was very quiet. A small girl by the door sniffled a bit, was perhaps crying, and I approved of the way Mrs. Harden bent down and stroked the girl's hair and talked quietly to her.

In the large classroom, which was to be Mike's, Mrs. Harden said, "This is Miss Rhonda. She has a degree in elementary education from Franklin University."

A young, stout, wholesome-looking woman, with round, pink cheeks and a cap of short brown hair shook my hand.

"What kind of things do you teach the children?" I asked Miss Rhonda.

"Oh, all sorts of things," she said promptly. There was no hesitation here, not with Miss. Rhonda. She pointed at a skinny boy in a corner.

"Danny over there is learning his alphabet," she said assertively. "And James here can now count to ten. He just started last week and didn't know any of his numbers then."

Mike had pulled out a plastic container of blocks from one of the shelves and started building a tower. Just then, a small, wiry, freckled boy grabbed one of Mike's blocks and threw it across the room. Another teacher, a tall, heavy African-American woman, an assistant, I assumed, immediately stepped in and scolded the freckle-faced boy.

"And you teach manners, don't you?" I asked.

"Oh definitely," said Miss Rhonda, a bit menacingly. I decided to ignore that hint.

The school seemed perfect. I quickly filled out a myriad of forms and wrote out a check for two month's tuition— one for a deposit, and the other for November and the rest of October. Mrs. Harden whisked all of this away into numerous, color-coded folders and files. I had agreed to start Mike the very next day, and even decided to enroll him until three in the afternoon, rather than until just noon, which I had originally planned. I was so sure he was going to like Forest Lane. Mike could have lunch and take a nap with the other children.

"I can stay with him tomorrow, right?" I asked. "Because I would like to do that."

"Of course," said Mrs. Harden with a wide smile. "The first days are always difficult. You can stay for as long as you like."

The school had been chosen then, and I would finally be able to start working again. Larry, startled that I had made up my mind so quickly, agreed to go in with us the next morning, so that he could see the school for himself and say goodbye to Mike.

But that night, I could not sleep. I felt restless and jittery and tried to read a book, but my brain would not rest, insisting on running down list after list of questions and concerns and what ifs and unhappy scenarios. Finally, I drifted off into an exhausted sleep, only to be jolted awake a few hours later by a nightmare. I had dreamed Mike had been staying with a babysitter and gotten scratched by a cat. In my dream, I saw the scratch—a long, jagged, ugly, red welt—only after it had already scabbed over. Mike had said he was fine, but I felt a terrible, overwhelming sadness I had not been there to comfort him when it happened.

We drove, the three of us, to the school that morning. The sky was a sleepy, cold, milk-white, undecided yet as to whether it would blossom into a clear, sunny day or remain wrapped up in its dreary, cottony cloudiness.

At the school, Mike cheerfully hung up his coat on the rack in the foyer, his usual optimistic self, certain that a good adventure was in store. For didn't Mommy always arrange fun things to do in the past? This whole preschool experience was just another exciting outing, he seemed to think, for even though Larry and I had carefully explained to him he would be staying at the school by himself, for nearly the whole day, I was not sure Mike understood the import of our words. He ran into the classroom, and Mrs. Rhonda greeted him briskly. They set about trying to find something for him to do. Larry and I stood in a corner, watching, and occasionally Mike would look over at us to make sure we were still there. There were about ten other children in the room, and two assistants I had not seen before—an immensely overweight lady with glasses, and a stringy, older lady who kept nagging at the children to do this or not to do that. When a little girl tried to climb on a low stool to look out the window, she angrily scolded her to come down, though as far as I could see, the girl wasn't harming anybody or herself. When another small child asked if he could get a drink, the old lady barked out a sharp "no," for some unknown reason. These small incidents set off an alarm in my mind, and I stored them away to tell Larry later.

Meanwhile, a skinny boy with shaggy, black hair tried to grab a toy car Mike was playing with. The boy was older and taller than Mike, but Mike had no problem yanking the car back and shouting, "Mine!" The older boy scurried away, looking frightened—unusually so, I thought. He wandered over dejectedly to the fat lady, whining softly, "Mike pushed me." I was about to protest, but then, I saw the woman had either not heard the boy or was, unbelievably, ignoring him.

The boy repeated once again, even more forlornly, "Mike hit me!"

And again, the stout lady stared stonily ahead of her, at what I am not sure, but she was intentionally ignoring him. Finally, the poor kid shuffled away. My indignation at the boy had faded by then. I felt sorry for him. There was something wrong with the hopeless tone of his voice and the sad slump of his thin shoulders—as if he had half expected to be ignored all along, as if this was the way of his life. And there was something definitely wrong with the heavy lady's willful refusal to acknowledge his presence or his complaint. I was about to relate this story to Larry, but he said he had to go, and that Mike seemed to be doing fine. Miss Rhonda also chose this time to approach us.

"You know, it's easier for the children if the parents leave right away," she said, brusquely. "I've been doing this for a long time, and it's always better that way."

"Oh, we were just about to go," I said, relieved to see Mike playing happily. "I'll be back at three to pick him up."

Miss Rhonda smiled reassuringly, "He'll be just fine. He's doing great. Most kids don't do this well on their first day. You can call during the morning to check up on him."

This was all that was needed to satisfy me. Larry and I hugged and kissed Mike, who did not seem at all concerned. This was too easy, I thought. Did Mike really understand he would be here by himself for several hours?

"Mommy will be back to pick you up in the afternoon," I told him, slowly and distinctly, holding onto both of his hands and making sure he was giving me his full attention. "After lunch, and after nap. You will be taking your nap here, okay?"

Mike said, "Okay Mommy. See you later." He tugged away, so that he could go back to playing with his cars.

We waved to him from the door and left. The door had a window in it, and we watched through this for a while, but Mike simply continued playing with his cars, and anyway, the ever-vigilant Miss Rhonda was standing nearby.

Larry went to work, and I, instead of conscientiously heading straight back home to my computer, made a detour to our town's outdoor mall. The morning had bloomed into a crisp, blue-skied fall day, cool and sunny, perfect for outside strolls. I was unable to concentrate, so soon after leaving Mike. I wanted to be ready to leave immediately if I got a call, and the mall was conveniently nearby, less than a mile away. So, I walked restlessly past the stores, now unencumbered by a little body or a baby bag. At ten o'clock, I called to check on him. Mrs. Harden answered the phone.

"He's just fine" she reported confidently. "He did cry a little bit, just for a few minutes, but he's playing outside now."

Reassured, I hung up and resumed my window shopping. See? I told myself. He's doing fine. You're silly to get all worked up about nothing. But I phoned again anyway, at eleven-thirty. Again, Mrs. Harden said he was "just fine."

"He's having lunch now," she informed.

"I'll call back in an hour," I said. "Because I'm not sure how he'll do at nap time. You will call me won't you if he cries a lot? I'll just come get him early."

"Oh of course," said Mrs. Harden. "Don't worry. We'll let you know."

I visited the bookstore, browsed through an art gallery, and looked at furniture, clothes, and shoes. Punctually, an hour later, I dialed up the school again.

Mrs. Harden said, "He cried a little bit, but now he's sleeping. He's had a good day. Don't worry."

"I'm so relieved," I said. "I'll be over soon to pick him up."

I was getting tired of the mall, but I didn't want to go home, since three o'clock was now only an hour away. I resisted giving the school another call or driving over too early to pick Mike up. I'm going to be strong, I told myself, even though I was missing him terribly and could not stop thinking about him. I sat down in a little coffee shop and slowly sipped a cappuccino and held a newspaper in front of my face. Finally, at two-thirty, I drove over.

Miss Rhonda was in the classroom by herself; the children were out on the playground.

"How was his day?" I asked her eagerly.

"He did well," she said, and then laughed as if about to relate a funny story. "You know, he was crying on and off throughout the day and I finally got him to stop. I said, 'you can't have a snack until you stop crying'!" Miss Rhonda looked very pleased with herself. I was shocked. This was their way of comforting a child on his first day of school, bribing him with snacks? And why hadn't Mrs. Harden told me he was "crying on and off" all day?

Miss Rhonda chattered on, "Oh, by the way, does he know how to use the potty?"

"No," I said. "Not yet, although we're working on it."

Miss Rhonda exclaimed triumphantly, "I *thought* so!" and rolled her eyes. She told me how Mike had said "potty" and she had asked him if he knew how to use one.

"When he told me 'yes,' I thought to myself, 'yeah, right'!" she nearly spat, and chuckled coldly.

I was, again, appalled by her manner, as if she had caught him in some kind of terrible crime. Mike is only two,

I wanted to remind her, and incapable of that kind of dishonesty. But I had a feeling she would not have agreed or understood. Her whole attitude was one of antagonism towards Mike, as if he were some juvenile delinquent trying to challenge her authority. Another warning sounded in my mind, this time about Miss Rhonda, but my first and more overwhelming concern was to find Mike. I ran outside towards the playground and was relieved to see him climbing the jungle gym, along with the other children. The African-American assistant I had seen on my first visit was supervising. I noticed there were actually two playgrounds, one small, shabby one and another larger, more attractive one. All the children were playing on the smaller playground. As soon as I appeared, Mike jumped off the jungle gym and ran towards the larger playground. He climbed up on the ladder towards the slide. All the children watched him as he did this, and one boy pointed at him.

"Miss Delilah," the boy shouted. "Mike's on the other playground!"

Why the children were not allowed on the bigger, more attractive jungle gym, I did not know, but as Mike was already at the top of the slide, I let him continue playing there. Meanwhile, I walked over to Miss Delilah to introduce myself. Although she looked large and forbidding, I wanted to get to know her, especially since it seemed she spent a good deal of time with the children. I also wondered why Miss Delilah had not been introduced to me in the first place.

"That your son?" she asked, nodding gravely towards Mike, and I said yes. She broke out into an unexpected, yellow-toothed grin.

"He's a very special boy," she said. "Very smart." And then suddenly her voice lowered, and a frown came over her face.

"You should take him out of here," she said. "This is a bad place." I was startled by her savage tone.

"Why do you say that?" I asked.

"The teachers are bad," she said, angrily. "They don't watch the children. I just started working here last week. As temporary help. And already I'm the only one with the children nearly the entire day."

I wasn't sure what to make of this—if I should believe her or not—but now that I had this information, I could not ignore it.

"Thank you for telling me," I said evenly, though I was very unnerved. "I'll probably stay tomorrow and observe for the whole day."

Miss Delilah nodded. "Your son is a special boy. Nice boy. And very smart. Take him out of here. Stay home with him."

I nodded dumbly and told Mike it was time to go home. Who *was* this Miss Delilah? She had a rough look about her and was obviously different from the other teachers and assistants. Could it be she was just a disgruntled employee, seeking revenge upon her employers? I did not know whether to believe her accusations or not, although her violent dissatisfaction was certainly a bad sign. I wondered why she kept saying Mike was special. I knew Mike was precocious, more articulate than most other children his age, but there was something else—and then I took a closer look at the kids on the playground, and I saw what she meant. Though the children ran about and played like normal children, there also seemed to be hints of unusual timidity, even neglect, about most of them—it was in their thin, pale limbs, in their shabby clothing, and especially, in the guarded, watchful, evasive, even fearful look in their eyes. It was the same look I had seen in the brown boy, the one who had tried half-heartedly to get the teaching assistant's attention. The constant rebukes I had seen in the classroom, the combative attitude of Miss Rhonda, the orderly efficiency of Mrs. Harden all now took on an ominous quality. No longer was this school a fairy-tale castle, so much as a prison or juvenile boot camp. This, I realized with some astonishment, was very much an adult-centered environment, hostile towards children. Thoughts like these turned slowly in my mind, and I think I had already decided at that point to take Mike out of the school—or maybe I even knew at the time Miss Rhonda spoke so disparagingly of him. Yet I did not act decisively. I had to have more evidence. I had to see for myself how

Mike's day really went. It made my heart ache terribly to think I had subjected him, for even one single day, to a place where he had been neglected or even treated badly—but I had to find out what was going on.

The next morning, I called to inform the school I would be staying to observe for the entire day. Miss Harden dismissively said that would be "just fine." Unfortunately, Larry was having trouble with his car, so we had to drop off Mike first, then drive Larry to work, and then I would have to drive back to the school by myself.

This time, when we arrived at Forest Lane, Mike did not eagerly bound in and he did not want to hang up his coat. He stood hesitatingly outside the classroom door.

"Come on, let's go in, Mike," said Larry, taking his hand.

"No," said Mike, though it wasn't a very strong refusal.

Miss Rhonda came out, and asked Mike if he would like to work on some puzzles? He seemed slightly interested, so we took him gently by the hand, and led him into the classroom. I saw, with some relief, that Miss Delilah was in the room this morning, reading, in a glowering yet also inexplicably gentle manner, to another child.

"I have to take Daddy to work, honey," I whispered to Mike. "And then I'm going to come back and stay with you at school. Okay?"

"Okay Mommy," he said, momentarily distracted by the wood puzzles.

Larry and I slipped out into the small classroom, adjoining Mike's classroom, so that we could watch Mike for a few minutes, through the window in the door. But there in the adjoining classroom, I experienced two alarming incidents simultaneously. While I was watching Mike through the window, Larry began a conversation with the large lady assistant, who was sitting at a low table next to two children—it was the same woman who had ignored the little boy yesterday. The children in this small classroom, one boy and one girl, were seated side by side, with exactly one paltry cracker square and one small paper cup of water set in front of them. Neither the boy nor the girl, I noticed, touched the food. They did not talk. They did not play with any of the toys in the room or near the table. They did not read. They did not look around or squirm or smile or frown. They did not, I observed with increasing alarm, do anything besides sit there with the most vacant and lifeless expressions I have ever seen. There was not even a hint of suppressed energy or restlessness or anger or any other kind of life in their faces; their expressions were simply zombie-like—whatever they were feeling, it was something way beyond boredom and hopelessness. The fat lady continued her droning conversation with Larry, who for some reason, conversed back, and then another assistant, the same old nag from yesterday, came in and sat down next to the children, on the other side. But just like the fat lady, she did not even glance at these living-dead children, much less speak to them. Finally, she got up and slapped down what looked like color charts on the table. The children did not look at the charts or even acknowledge the woman's presence. At the same time, I was witnessing this disturbing scene, I was also peeking through the window into Mike's classroom—and was subjected to another heart-wrenching sight. My own little Mike had discovered we were gone and was screaming and crying. He got up from the "circle time" which had commenced at nine, and repeatedly tried to take his little sweater off one of the coat racks in the room, in an attempt to "go home."

"Daddy! Daddy!" sobbed Mike, and the two women sitting at the table next to us smiled.

"Oh, they're always like that," said the fat one.

Fortunately, Miss Delilah took Mike over to a table, and let him sit on her lap. He was still crying, but at least she was trying to read to him and comfort him. I wanted to go in there and grab Mike, but I did not. The assistants next to us, at the table with the zombie children, continued smiling at Mike's crying, and I resisted the urge to slap their stupid faces. Surely this could not be a normal situation. My mind was frozen, and I felt unreal and sick. Larry had to leave for work, so we finally walked out towards the car, leaving Mike, still crying in Delilah's lap. We talked about what we had seen but Larry was strangely cool and calm. Probably I would have gone in and taken Mike, if Larry had encouraged it. But I am sure he was thinking that all children cried during their first separation from their parents—just because Mike was crying, did not mean Forest Lane was a bad school. But then again, he hadn't seen what I had seen, and didn't know what I knew. It would be up to me to "save" Mike, for that was ridiculously, how I was viewing this whole situation now—as a rescue mission.

I arrived back at the school about half an hour later, after what was both the longest and fastest drive in my life. On my way to the classroom, I ran directly into Mrs. Harden, who, to my astonishment, seemed upset at my re-appearance.

"It's not a good idea to stay around while he is getting adjusted," she said severely. I wondered what happened to their open-door policy. It was incomprehensible to me that she had lied about that. But then I understood, suddenly, she had not really expected me to stay. The school probably told all the parents that it had an open-door policy—and then none of the parents actually ever visit, because all felt falsely confident, he or she could do so at any time. I could not, however, believe a school could be so brazenly dishonest.

"Oh, but I told you I was going to stay this morning," I said sweetly. "And here I am!" I gave her an innocent smile and proceeded calmly into the classroom.

I was beginning to feel as if I was breaking into some sort of concentration camp, and I was growing increasingly, exponentially worried. I was relieved to see the children in the classroom, milling around Miss Delilah. The room was darkened, and Miss Rhonda was nowhere to be seen. When Mike saw me, he ran and clung to my legs as if they were life preservers. I pried his hands off and told him he could sit with me.

"I'm going to stay the whole day," I reassured him. His confidence returned and he sat, smiling, on my lap.

"They said I could," I informed Miss Delilah, in case she should give me some trouble too. "I asked about it this morning."

Miss Delilah came over, nodding vigorously. "It's good you're here," she said, with that same dark voice as yesterday, with the bitter anger boiling just beneath the surface. "Then you'll see what goes on here! This is the worst place I've ever worked at! The teachers are never here! I am with the children the entire day! You'll see."

I sat, numbed by this additional outburst, and tried to think of what to do. But the nightmare only worsened. Miss Delilah had managed to corral the children into a silent circle, and then turned on a record player, which blasted out some of the most discordant "children's" music I had ever heard. The children sat silently, neither moving nor talking. They stared dumbly into space, with no trace of enjoyment, or any kind of feeling in their faces—how could they endure such loud and ugly music? They were just like the zombie children, and this was another horrifying spectacle. Just then, the door was flung open, and Mrs. Orne appeared in the lighted doorway. I was shocked yet again. Mrs. Orne had been transformed. She was no longer the kindly, grandmotherly woman from the kitchen, but a huge, white-haired demon, a wicked witch from the forest.

"Mrs. Zhang!" she boomed, in a strange, rough voice. "Come with me!"

Could it be possible she was talking to me in this way? As if I was—a *child*? I stood up, and said, not nicely. "What do you want?"

"We would like to talk to you in the office!" she menaced. "Leave your son here!"

"I will certainly not leave him here," I retorted, scooping up Mike and following her out of the room. Miss Delilah and the rest of the children stared longingly after us as we left. It was the last time we saw them.

The three of us filed into Mrs. Harden's office. Mrs. Harden was seated behind her desk as usual, and there was another lady, someone I hadn't seen before, standing next to her. This new lady was plump, well-groomed, iron-haired, and middle-aged, and she wore a luxurious, sleek, black fur coat. She carried herself as though she was someone very important; and didn't want anyone to forget about it. Next to her, Mrs. Harden looked positively meek.

"This is Mrs. Schwartz, the owner," nodded Mrs. Orne solemnly, and she sat down in one of the chairs as if she was some kind of gang leader, about to pronounce judgment on a traitorous member.

"Mrs. Harden tells me you have not been observing the rules," said Mrs. Schwartz crisply. "She says that you want to stay here all day to observe. We don't allow that. It disturbs the children."

"I was told I could come here at any time to observe," I replied calmly. "And I made clear to Mrs. Harden this morning I would be staying the whole day today."

"That is not possible," Mrs. Schwartz said.

"I must see how my son spends his days here."

"We've *never* had this problem before," pressed Mrs. Schwartz. "*Nobody* has ever requested to stay the whole day. We can't allow it."

"And if you can't abide by the rules," Mrs. Orne threatened. "You will have to leave."

"Then I will," I said dramatically, even though of course I had already made up my mind much earlier. The three women, however, were taken aback.

"You agreed to enroll him until the spring," reminded Mrs. Harden. "I won't be able to give you your deposit back."

"That's fine," I said, overcome with a desperate urge to get out of there. "I was going to start him at another school anyway in the spring."

This was exactly the wrong thing to say. Mrs. Schwartz stood up and her face turned red. I almost expected her to stamp her foot.

"You," she spluttered, "were going to take him out of *my* school, so that he could go to another school!"

I could not imagine why she was upset at this, and her righteous attitude threw me off. I was obviously not going to get anywhere with these people.

"I don't think this is the right time for us to start Mike."

Mrs. Orne softened a bit, and said, "Oh it's always harder for the parents," she said. "The kids always cry for the first few days. I know one mother whose son cried every day for three weeks! But they always get over it."

I shuddered, for certainly, that was true—the children did get "over it"—because they had given up all hope that anybody would rescue, or even listen to them.

"And your son was doing so well yesterday," Mrs. Orne continued. "He only cried for a few hours."

It was my turn to stand up. For a few hours! Mike had never cried for a few hours in his life, not even as an infant! They had reassured me that he had only been "crying on and off." I felt ill, not only at their dishonesty, but also by the fact that while I had been out enjoying myself yesterday, poor Mike had been here, miserable, crying "for hours"!

I picked up Mike and rushed out the door without another word.

Half a year later, and after three more failed attempts at other schools, Mike finally enrolled at the small Montessori school I had liked in the beginning. Happily, he stayed there for three years. It wasn't perfect, and I did not always agree with his teacher or the director, but I did trust them. After that, I taught Mike myself at home.

I didn't forget the children at Forest Lane. I called the state licensing department and a woman promised to do a surprise visit on the school, but that was all she could do. There had been no previous complaints about the school. The last time I read about Forest Lane—in an ad in the local parenting paper—they were due to open a new location in another nearby town.

K I T E

Karen and her eight-year-old son, Evan, were walking along the upland trail at James Abbey Park, a two-point-one-mile gravel path that circled wetlands and prairie. It was a warm and windy autumn day, with the bright blue skies of gorgeous Indian summer. Evan, of course, was not really walking—he was running, running, running, back and forth along the path with his kite—a navy-blue and white rectangular-shaped Parafoil, with splendid navy, white, and scarlet streamers—shouting with joy as the strong wind swooped it up high into the wide blue sky, and then dropped it back down again—only to lift it up once more, higher and higher, until it was a mere shining disk next to the sun. It took all of Evan's strength to hold onto the string as the wind, like a powerfully giant child, tugged capriciously back. Karen helped Evan maneuver the kite around a few trees that stood along the path, but mostly, there was wide-open space—the kite flew up and down, around and around, unfettered, higher and higher into the atmosphere. The smell of cut grass and leaves, the tangy smoke from a distant bonfire added to the delightfulness of the afternoon. It seemed like all the stress from the past few months, all the ambivalence and angst surrounding their trouble-ridden move from California had melted away with the balmy, golden sunshine.

This wasn't the first time they had brought the kite out to the park. When they had moved to town in mid-October, Evan had right away wanted to try out the kite in the wide, flat fields, so unlike the Southern California landscape he had grown up with. Karen thought it would be a good way to adjust to the strangeness of Iowa and take Evan's mind off of California, although he did not appear to be missing the West very much. She had described Iowa in such glowing detail, for one thing, that to a happy-go-lucky and imaginative child such as Evan, the entire move was quite simply an enormous adventure.

'Will there be snow in Iowa?" was the most urgent question, and to this, Karen could reply with a definite affirmative. "Oh yes, Evan, there will be snow. There will be a *lot* of snow."

So, there was all the excitement of snow, of a new place, and although a more knowledgeable, older person might have viewed Iowa as an undesirable destination, to Evan, it held all the glamour and pizzazz of a New York City. Plenty of open space and strong wind to fly kites materialized as an unanticipated benefit, and Karen made good use of this. During the first few sessions at the park, she had been worried there would not be enough wind, or maybe the kite would get stuck in the faraway, large trees, but none of these things had happened. Instead, everything had gone perfectly—maybe too perfectly. Even when there had not been quite enough wind along the main paths bordering the lake, they were able to fly the kite for short distances on the upland trail. Both Karen and Evan felt that Evan was entirely an expert with the kite—nothing could possibly go wrong. When the first frost came a few weeks later, they were disappointed, but satisfied they had at least gotten in some kite-flying, even during a season not normally known for good kite-weather.

Then came today, one more beautiful day, with mild breezes and sunshine. They thought they should take the kite out one last time before winter finally came.

They had no problem getting the kite up into the sky, as usual, once they started up the broad hill past the trailhead. But then they came towards the grove of very old, established oaks and maples near the crest of the trail—tall and thick, fat and full of dying leaves, standing close together. Brambly bushes and tall, prickly grass grew all around, forming a low barricade. From a distance, the grove looked pleasantly shady, almost inviting, but here, up close, anyone would have second thoughts about attempting to hack through all that brush. As usual, they maneuvered easily around the more isolated trees, but when they came upon the grove, Karen offered to take the kite's string and fly it around the "danger zone."

"Well, okay," said Evan.

"Just until we get around these trees."

She took the string and was surprised by how strong the wind was, how much the kite pulled and pulled. Maybe a bit more string would get the kite above the trees. She released the string, a little at a time. This seemed to work, and Evan shouted the kite was about to clear the trees. But then the wind stopped, dropping the kite several feet from its safe spot in the sky, and blew it into the opposite direction. The kite veered towards the dark grove, the string drawing an ominous curve in the sky. Karen started pulling the kite down, thinking she could reel it in before it caught in the branches, but she wasn't fast enough. The wind picked up the kite and blew it straight towards the tallest tree; for a moment, it swung the kite away from the tree and she thought it was going to clear it—but then no. The kite stuck to one of the highest branches. Without its leaves in that one particular spot, the tree limbs looked delicate and skeletal, holding onto the kite as if it were some dainty handkerchief; when Karen gave the kite a few quick pulls, the branches held on quite stubbornly. Evan let out a loud, distressed wail. In his blue and silver baseball jacket, baggy khakis, and matching cap, he looked small and furiously helpless.

"We'll get it out," Karen said, trying not to panic. *Of course, you'll get the kite down*, she told herself. *Of course, you will. Calm down.*

She tugged again at the kite, as Evan watched with wide, teary eyes. *His favorite kite. It was his favorite kite. Eighty bucks at that Seaport Village shop on the Harbor.* On and on the self-reproaches ran in her mind, faster and faster. *They shouldn't have come out here today. They shouldn't have brought the kite. They could've just taken a walk. Why hadn't she just stayed away from the trees. Why had they come to Iowa? No one would help them. They were alone. She was alone.*

"Maybe we could throw something to knock it down," she suggested, trying to keep from breaking down into tears herself. They looked around, and then, at the tree. The kite was caught up so high, she knew nothing they threw would reach anywhere near the top. Even so, they tossed a few useless sticks at it.

Karen gave the kite a few more quick pulls, and for a moment, it looked as if the branches would release its prey, but the kite just fell down to another branch and stuck fast again. Evan tried pulling at it, and then Karen again. The string broke.

"Oh Evan," Karen said, "I'm so sorry. I'll call the park office and see if any of the rangers can help us get it down." She dialed information on her cell, which directed her, unexpectedly, to a live person.

"I'm sorry," the woman said, after Karen's very long-winded, very jumbled account of the ordeal, ending with a plea for help in getting the kite down. "The rangers don't do that kind of thing."

"Could I leave my name and phone number with you, in case it falls out and someone happens to find it?"

"Sure."

It made Karen feel better to be doing something, although she had almost zero hope that she would get a call about the kite. If someone found it, they would probably keep it. She was pretty sure that was what usually happened.

A few people walking along the path stared at the two of them, looking up at the tree—none offered to help, although a few showed some curiosity.

"Our kite is stuck," she told a couple cutting across the fields, a young man and woman in jeans and matching T-shirts. They both smiled and walked on. Again, Karen felt like crying, although she understood they thought it was just a funny child's thing that happened. Just a kite stuck in a tree.

"It's like in Peanuts, with Charlie Brown," she said. "A kite-eating tree."

Evan shouted, "Stupid tree! Stupid, stupid tree!" He ran over to kick the trunk, but had a hard time getting through all the brambles.

There was nothing more they could so. After wandering back and forth in front of the tree for some time, looking up to see if the wind would bring it back out of the branches, they decided to come back the next day and try hitting it out of the tree with a tennis ball or bow and arrow. Karen caught hold, tightly, of Evan's cold hand, and they went home.

Karen and Evan had moved to Iowa because that was where Karen had grown up, where she had gone to college, and where her childhood friend, Lynn, still lived and worked. They moved to Iowa because costs were low there, the housing was inexpensive, one could get a four-bedroom house with yard backing to woods for the same price as a cramped eight-hundred square foot apartment in Orange County. Living expenses were just getting too high for them in Southern California, on her office manager's salary she couldn't really afford even their tiny apartment, couldn't afford the private school Evan had attended since he was three, and Evan was growing older now, maybe he needed more space to run around, and for his toys and projects. From her research, Karen knew the schools in Sheridan were of good quality, as far as public schools went. The neighborhoods would be safe, and he could make some new friends, maybe just as she and Lynn had become friends and stayed in touch all these long, long years.

The timing seemed right.

For example, Evan was set to "transition" to a new upper-elementary class next year at Solana Hills Montessori, having just completed the first three-year cycle of the lower-elementary program. He was prepared for a new set of classmates. Sheridan, unfortunately, did not have any Montessori schools—the options were limited to the local public schools and to a few small, private Catholic schools—but Lynn had reassured Karen over the course of her information-gathering sessions that her own son,

Jeremy, two years older than Evan, was doing very well and enjoying the sixth grade at one of the local Sheridan schools.

No doubt, they were going to miss Solana Hills—its spacious green parks, wide streets, and new apartment buildings and shopping centers. She had enjoyed taking walks with Evan along Bells Cove Beach, looking for starfish and sea urchins, watching the tide come in. They would miss reading books at the cozy Solana Hills Public Library. Karen had made friends with some of the moms of Evan's friends, but none of these were like the long friendship she had with Lynn. She liked the other moms, but if it weren't for Evan, she probably wouldn't be hanging out with them. Most of them were just out of her financial league. She couldn't talk about large houses, or vacations, or boarding schools. There was one woman she had grown to like very much, but she moved to Virginia, where her husband had relatives—the woman said she had grown tired of Solana Hills. *It's too neat and perfect here*, she had said. *Like a bubble.* The words stuck with Karen. She thought of a giant, clear-coated plastic bubble roof filling the blue sky, covering the entire town—not allowing her to get out.

Logically, she knew the bubble was an illusion. She could get out. She was not a child, stuck in a basement bedroom, dependent upon the whims of her parents. Most of all, there was nothing—and no one—holding her here in Solana Hills anymore.

The next day was still warm, although not as sunny. Armed with tennis rackets and tennis balls, Karen and Evan went back to Abbey Park. The kite was still in the tree. After hitting a few balls up into the air—she almost nicked it one time—they had to give up because the kite was too high up in the branches. You can always go back and visit it, Lynn joked, they next time they got together for a Sunday dinner. Karen had been hoping Lynn would offer to help her get it down, or that at least, Lynn's husband, Joe, would help them. The first few times Joe and Lynn had come over to visit Karen and Evan, Joe had inspected the entire house and offered to fix everything broken he came across—and that had been a lot of things.

I can take care of that, he would say, *just a couple of nails should do it.* Or, *that needs to be re-wired. I can do it.*

She found herself a little jealous of Lynn. Joe took care of things. He and Jeremy went camping and fishing and hunting. He chopped wood. Sometimes, he cooked dinner. A few times, early on, Lynn asked Karen and Evan if they would like to go camping with them. But the camping trip never materialized. It seemed, to Karen, that the good will between them was fading, but she did not know how to stop it, didn't know what to do to make things better—back to the way it was when they were children. She had thought her friendship with Lynn was simply too strong to come apart like this.

But up close, she began to see the reality. She and Lynn had grown apart in almost every way possible. They were no longer two nine-year-old girls in the same class, riding bikes and baking cookies together at Lynn's house on the weekends. Karen became impatient with Lynn for not spending more time with her and Evan, and Lynn was a little suspicious of Karen, a newly single mom arrived from a not very well-grounded place like California, an unstable type who didn't go to church.

Even deeper than that: Lynn was suspicious that Joe was paying too much attention to Karen, suspicious her single friend was maybe after Joe. Or was this only Karen being— dare she say it—paranoid? If only Lynn knew how unfounded such fears were, if she ever did, in fact, possess them. Joe helped Karen because he was a generous person and he loved Lynn. If it ever came down to it, Joe would completely stop helping Karen, stop showing up at their dinners and outings together if Lynn wanted it that way. She was amazed at this kind of husbandly devotion.

Karen met Dan, Evan's father, during one of those hazy college parties she and her roommates sometimes attended on Friday or Saturday nights, sick of studying and wanting to dance and just meet some cute guys. Dan was a friend of her roommate, Carrie, and as soon as he and Karen were introduced, there was an immediate physical attraction. She was an awestruck and naive freshman, Dan a self-assured senior and star math major. They dated for a few months, and although Dan continued to see other girls, Karen thought of it as a serious romance. Dan was everything she thought she wanted it in a man—extremely smart, well-liked, handsome, an eloquent speaker. Perhaps he was a bit of a snob, but she forgave him this because he was so sophisticated and intelligent. He never mistreated her, but neither did he ever say he loved her or show her generous affection. Karen was busy with her classes and work at the physics library, so she did not suspect Dan was trying to get rid of her, thought she was too needy. As it turned out, things worked out for him because he graduated and simply left Sheridan one day, after accepting a job offer in California. Karen knew where his job was, but he did not tell her when he left. By that time, she was already pregnant with Evan.

"So, did you ever talk to Dan while you were in California?" asked Lynn, at a Friday night pizza dinner—sans Joe—shortly after the kite-flying incident. Lynn knew all about what happened between Karen and Dan, how Karen had sort of followed Dan out to Southern California after she graduated with an English degree, without ever once calling him or telling him about the baby. He had not tried to contact her either, although she had stayed in the same apartment long after he left. She thought she would just wait until she got a job, was settled, and could prove she was able to take care of the both herself and the baby, without Dan's help. Maybe that didn't make sense to everyone who knew about her situation, but that's how she wanted it.

"No," said Karen, almost apologetically. "He would've wanted to talk to me." Actually, she had long lost his address and knew he didn't work at the same company anymore. She didn't know where Dan was, just somewhere in California. She tried to remember the name of the town he might be in, but she found her mind wandering, distracted by how messy her kitchen looked, how messy she and Evan probably looked in their shorts and sweatshirts. What were they doing wearing shorts in November anyway? And Evan's dark-brown hair was already hanging in his eyes and down the middle of his neck, definitely needing a haircut. He had said he wanted to grow it out, but it didn't look right. She wondered how boys were supposed to grow their hair out, if they needed maintenance cuts or something. Talking about haircuts, she had gone probably a few years without one, and now always wore it in a messy ponytail. In contrast, Lynn looked cool and professional with her short, blonde bob, and her work clothes—a silk shirt and gray pants. Jeremy had inherited Lynn's blond hair and looked positively the stereotypical Iowa boy—blue eyes, crewcut, freckles, a little chunky.

"Don't you think he would want to know about Evan?"

"No. I don't think he would."

Lynn shrugged, but appeared a little grim-faced. "I just can't understand that," she said. Karen knew what she meant, that a child should grow up with two parents.

Karen did grow up with two parents. Her father was an orthopedic surgeon and her mother was a bookkeeper. Both were extremely religious and did not approve of many of Karen's interests, which centered upon reading fairy tales and drawing imaginary creatures. In fourth grade, her teacher secretly submitted one of her drawings to a state-wide contest. She won first prize—a silver dollar and kept the coin for years in an old Christmas card box. Her father hadn't reacted (or perhaps even heard) when she told him of the award, and her mother wouldn't speak to Karen for a week, because Karen had dedicated the story to her father, and not to her. Unfortunately, the box with her award disappeared after she left for college. She didn't remember why she hadn't taken the box with her. She hadn't taken any of her childhood belongings. Everything, eventually, seemed to have just vanished.

After winning the contest, Karen began spending more and more time reading books checked out from the school library, but her foster parents put a stop to it—or they tried to. They banned Karen from reading fiction and instructed her teachers to "keep an eye" on her. *She's turned into such a dishonest child*, they told her teachers. *She won't listen to us. She spends all her time reading nonsense.* The only teacher who complied and actually "turned Karen in" was a math teacher, who disliked her. Karen still sneaked books home anyway and put them under her bed. Karen's parents sometimes found the hidden cache and, with an apparent lack of creativity, hid the books under their own bed. This Karen knew because when they weren't home, she would sneak into their room and discover them. Sometimes she would take the books back and then she would be punished and have to stand in a corner for an entire afternoon. They would call her "stupid" for reading such trash, and "evil" for lying about having the trash in the first place.

After Karen went to college, her parents moved away from Iowa and settled in a suburb outside of San Francisco. They were furious when Karen told them about Evan, and she did not hear from them again, and nor did she try to contact them. However, she knew that her foster mother had an unmarried, much older sister in Southern California, a gentle and soft-spoken woman who had always encouraged Karen and sent birthday gifts. This aunt was a professor at a small, private college, and helped Karen and Evan get settled in the Southern California. Aunt Emily was only able to spend a year with them before she died suddenly one day from a heart attack. Karen and Evan were left alone again. But Aunt Emily had left them some money, and this enabled them to stay in one place a bit longer.

Karen and Evan, did, in fact, visit the kite. She didn't think that they would want to go back to that park, but it was the only decent park around, with its muddy man-made lake and swampy, puddly marshes, the tall prairie grass and wide fields. They went back, and Karen felt the same fear and guilt when she saw the kite, twisting in the trees or lying lethargically on windless days. She had thought about what it was, a few nights after the kite had gotten lost. Tried to identify that feeling she had. Fear, yes. But of what exactly? The feeling was familiar. *It was a sign*, she thought. *A sign that you will never get out of here. You and Evan stuck here forever.*

She had voluntarily come back to this place, tried to choose a house full of windows, so that it would be different from the kind of place she had been in before—in the basement. Her bedroom as a child had been in the basement, without windows. *You will never get out of here.* Those were the words that had often repeated themselves in her mind, as she lay in her bed at night, the night-light casting an orange glow upon the white-painted, cement-brick walls. Sometimes she heard mice scrabbling across the sheet of clear plastic covering the fluorescent lights above, and in the summer, shiny black crickets crawled along the walls, illuminated by the night-light. This was the basement after all, and the house was by the fields—nothing could keep these creatures out. But she never really got used to it.

Still, it had seemed normal, growing up—a bedroom in the basement, no windows, mice and crickets running around. Her best friend Lynn had even been over and seen her windowless room, had seemed to think nothing of it.

The extra bedroom in the basement was originally made—so her parents said—for an office. But her father had chosen the room on the other end of the basement, a larger one with two windows.

Their current house in Sheridan was nothing like her childhood home—which was a hundred miles away, anyway, in another small town close to the Illinois border—and yet, the former tenant who had shown her the house had even told her, *I thought the landlords were slumlords when I first saw this place.* He had chosen it for its privacy, its large, elaborately landscaped yard that backed to the woods, the floor to ceiling windows that looked out upon them. This was the reason Karen had chosen it as well. And Evan—he had loved the house when they first moved in. Right away he had set up his room with all of his stuffed animals, his Lego projects, his special collections of stones and sticks. They didn't notice the cracked, aging linoleum, the bumpy kitchen countertops, the outlets that would not work, the peeling paint on the porch. Karen had not noticed this or had not paid attention.

Winter came finally, an unusually snowy and long one. Karen was busy with her new job as a secretary at the university, and Evan was doing well at the local school, where he had made a few friends. After the snows came, she and Evan rented cross-country skis and tried skiing at the golf course, instead of taking their usual walks. Lynn came over with Jeremy on Friday nights for pizza dinners. Joe, however, completely stopped showing up. *He's at the office,* Lynn would say. Or, *he's working on the spare bedroom/plumbing/paperwork at home.*

Karen and Evan looked less and less for the kite when they went walking on the paths, and after the heavy snows, there seemed to be no point. Snow and ice would have ruined it. Still, she hoped each time they passed the group of trees that one day, she would get it out of there. *It will fall out,* she thought, *or the tree branches will snap and let it go. A heavy wind in the springtime will lift it out of the trees.*

The spring was brief and mild, but summer was a different story. One of the worst storms in Sheridan's history occurred one night in mid-June. There had been plenty of thunderstorms during their time in town, which she had not gotten used to, even having lived all those childhood and college years in Iowa. But this storm—she had been really frightened at the way the lightening went on and on, without stop, without sound, just flash, after blue-white flash, lighting up the black trees from the woods, like a crazy camera. The wind was tremendous, blowing the trees back and forth, but again, there was no sound, no thunder. The flashes went on and on, and finally the thunder arrived, cracking the sky in two, it seemed. But mostly it was the lightning that was awful, the way it was so bright, so blindingly bright, beating out all the other senses with its ugly silent brightness. She closed her eyes to shut it out and still she could see the lightening through her lids.

Stop it, stop it, she whispered through clenched teeth—because it seemed the skies were screaming. During the night, she heard a crash outside, but thought it must be the grill that had been knocked off the porch. Thankfully, Evan slept through the entire storm. She sat beside him, in his room, watching the flashes in the sky until they gradually faded. Then she fell asleep on the floor.

The crash had been from a maple tree, planted too close to the house, which had split in two and had fallen to the ground, fortunately opposite the house. Otherwise the roof would have surely been damaged, or windows broken.

She could not believe the devastation she witnessed around town—hundreds of trees down, houses with their roofs bashed in. Yards with small mountains of debris to be picked up by the city trucks.

It was not long before she and Evan ventured to the park to take their walk. They had not looked for the kite for some time now. They felt that it was still there in the trees—Evan had more than once assured her he had seen a glimpse of navy blue in the branches. They felt that it had somehow survived the ice and snow, the spring rains—but what would happen to it in a storm like this? Large trees blocked the trails every few feet, and when they had stepped over several, and ducked under others, they came to the grove. The tree was now lying on its side, in the brambles, of course, for the prickly things had all grown back.

There was no sign of the kite. She was not surprised, but the old fear came back again, along with variations of the same old words. *You weren't able to save it. If she had only tried harder to save it.*

"Evan, it's not here anymore," she said, trying to clear away some of the branches. Evan stubbornly kicked away the nettles and brush, and they seemed to stick to him like so many ghastly hands, scratching at his face and hands. "Come back here, Evan. Please."

"Mom, I know it's here," he said.

"Evan."

"Just a few more minutes, Mom."

Half an hour later, he held it up. A torn navy and scarlet streamer.

They were in calm sunshine, the sand was soft and cool under their bare feet, and the Pacific surf was gentle today, as it washed over the beach. She and Evan were safe now, back again in familiar surroundings, and as the days passed, the bad memories began to fade. Still, sometimes, Karen permitted herself to think back on the other time, the other park from six months ago, and it seemed like it had just been a bad dream, as if they had stepped out of a sinister, mirror image of their life, and back into the real world. Only a shadow of a memory was left now—a tiny, bright, navy and white rectangle imprinted in black—and the feeling of loss and sorrow over the kite, left tattered and in pieces, to be blown away, bit by bit, by storms and wind, until there was nothing left behind.

THE YELLOW CURTAIN,
THE RED FLOOR

This is the kitchen, and yellow curtains hang in the window, framing the milky sky and pale-brown fields. A warm breeze blows back the curtains, because the window is open and because it is summer. Here she stands, in front of the window, at the sink, peeling potatoes and carrots for supper. Washing cups and plates, leftover from the younger children's afternoon snack. The girl's dreaming, and yet anxious, knowing that her mother will be home soon. There is so much left to do.

Here is the floor, an expanse of thin, dark-red carpet, patterned to look like tiles. The house was built seven years ago, in 1970—this carpet was the fashion then. The girl hates this carpet, hates the ugly red color, the squares inked on in black, the many, many hundreds of squares. These squares she scrubs, every afternoon, on hands and knees, with a rag and detergent—just so—because this is the only way to get them clean, or so she is told. She scrubs three squares a day, until the red color starts to bleed out of the fabric—and yet, the next day, when it's all dry, doesn't it all look just the same, just as dark and red as ever. It's stupid, it's pathetic. All that scrubbing, and just as red and ugly as before.

Maybe that's why her mother makes her do this. Some people are just like that. Sometimes the girl thinks her raw knees are what keep this disgusting carpet—her mother's carpet—so damn red. The girl scrubs and scrubs, hating and yet mesmerized by the infinite number of red squares that crawl over the kitchen floor, all over the living room, down the hallway. When she is done for the day, she rinses the rag at the kitchen sink, even though her mother has told her to do this in the laundry room sink. But her mother isn't home yet, so who cares? The breeze, now cooler, blows back the thin, yellow curtains, and the girl imagines herself floating away through the open window, hovering over the fields, flying away over the distant treetops.

She remembers the bread. It's a brand-new loaf kept in one of the cupboards. Stealthily she slides two slices out, from the middle of the crinkling, plastic bag—you can hardly tell they're missing. She's saving these for later, or perhaps for the next time she has a chance to get away.

The rumbling sound of the garage door fills the air. The girl quickly tucks the slices of bread into her sleeves—her mother calls it *stealing* when the girl takes food from the kitchen, outside of meals. Which, of course, doesn't make any sense.

There is a click, when the door to the garage opens. The kitchen light is turned on.

The girl stands in front of the window, waiting, framed by the gently blowing, yellow curtains. The sky outside is darkening, and the red carpet beneath her feet is damp and glowing, underneath the fluorescent lights.

Carrie was home for spring break, and the first thing she did was drive down to her favorite park, Torrey Pines State Beach and Reserve. The tide was high and there were several groups of people—families, tourists, a parade of joggers—already filling the beach, so she continued up the hill, towards the farthest parking lot. Today she would hike the entire North Tamarack Trail, the longest, steepest, least-traveled path, a little- known and difficult-to-find trail she had never been able to complete before. There was time today, and what was more, she felt it was the right moment to fulfill such a long-desired goal. In her backpack, she had brought an apple, chocolate bar, cheese sandwich, thermos of black coffee, and small, blank notebook—she planned on walking very slowly, taking long breaks on the lookout benches, so that she could watch all the birds, flowers, the sky, and ocean views, for as long as she wanted to. There was even a mysterious nature center at the end of the trail few people ever visited, the Arthur S. Hayward Center—she would go there today. As it was still relatively early, the sun lay calm, cool, and gray upon the sandy paths, the expanse of sagebrush and canyons was silent except for the occasional low call of a morning dove. After the busy school year, it was such a relief not to be in a hurry, not to have to rush anywhere, meet a deadline, or get ready for work.

When she had arrived home last night, her parents seemed glad to see her, and heaped upon her snacks—pretzels and Girl Scout cookies—and little flurries of attention. Her father was looking thinner, grayer, and shorter than she last remembered, and even her mother appeared like a slightly shrunken version of herself. For as long as Carrie could remember, her mother had always had the same short and curly hairstyle, except probably now it was dyed to resemble its original blue-black color. For dinner. Carrie's younger sister, Eva, picked up a pizza along her way home from work, and afterwards, they all watched the news, drank tea, and ate fruit and cookies together.

Later that night, while she and her sister were alone downstairs watching an old sit-com, Carrie asked Eva why her parents hadn't told her about—or invited her to—their Grandfather's funeral last month. Eva said she didn't know. Eva had accompanied their parents to the funeral in Lydia, a large city in Malaysia, which was their hometown. Instead she talked at length about how their parents had argued with their mother's siblings over the inheritance. *They really stood up for themselves*, Eva said excitedly. *I thought they were going to get into a fight.* Regarding these unexpected details Carrie, felt alarmed and confused. Their family almost never interacted with the particular uncle who ended up inheriting everything—Carrie had only seen his family once in the past decade and a half. Eva finally told Carrie how their Grandfather was buried next to their Grandmother in a beautiful mountainside cemetery, just outside of Lydia.

Along the way to the trail, Carrie admired the views from various lookout points, all of which were facing the ocean, vast and sparkling, as with stars. She passed several groves of Torrey Pines, their thick, twisted branches, contorted in fantastical formations.

"These are the rarest pines in the world," she had read somewhere, "They can be found only in this area of Southern California. They've adapted themselves successfully to the environment, bending their branches to the constant winds from the ocean." She tried to learn more about these trees, with their blackened and flattened shapes, but never could find a satisfactory answer as to why they really looked so unusual—for after all, did not harsh and strong winds occur almost everywhere on this earth? Why did they only look like this there, in this part of the world? Perhaps it was the sandy soil, which she thought she had also read about somewhere. Or the combination of cooling winds and proximity to the ocean. Maybe it was all of these things.

Carrie had only visited her hometown twice after coming to America. The first time, she was seven or eight. There had been a very hot car ride to the beach—her uncle driving, her aunt next to him, and she squeezed in between her sister and her mother in the back seat of the VW Bug—followed by a frightening swim in a very warm, immense, and salty ocean. The next scene she could recall was her grandparents' house in the city, with its red door leading into a small courtyard and large, dim, cool rooms. There had been a narrow kitchen, where her great-grandmother had chopped vegetables and prepared all sorts of delicious dishes. In the evenings, they all drank tea and ate cookies and watermelon upstairs and watched historical soap operas. Her grandmother had been a forbidding and imperious presence then, and Carrie had been a bit afraid of her. She did not know who this grand lady was, whom everyone, including her own mother, seemed to be so afraid of.

But these were only the scenes she could remember, that early on. There were others before that—what she had been told—she only learned about much later.

And the most important was this: her parents had moved to the United States a few months after she was born, without Carrie—her grandparents had taken care of Carrie for the first three years of her life. Eva was born in North Carolina, and the family had all moved to Illinois four years later. Carrie hadn't known her parents were not her first caretakers until her father mentioned it casually a few years ago. It had been "family night" and they were watching a movie about an adopted little girl when Carrie suddenly wondered aloud what she had been like at that age. Her mother was silent, but her father hesitated and then said he didn't know—they hadn't taken care of her as a toddler. Both sets of grandparents had watched over Carrie in Malaysia, although she had spent the majority of time with her maternal grandparents. When she had expressed her extreme surprise at this news, her father had acted surprised, too, and merely laughed, "Oh, I thought you knew?" They had rarely ever talked about her grandparents—and definitely had not, until now, ever connected her to Carrie's childhood. More than once, she asked her mother why they hadn't just left her in Malaysia with her relatives—after all, Carrie was reminded countless times over the years how difficult it had been for her mother to raise the two of them. Sometimes her mother said Carrie's grandparents were too sick and old to take care of a little baby, and other times, she ignored Carrie and started talking about something else. Over the following years, though, Carrie tried to piece together what had really happened, mostly from other relatives she managed to locate through social media. Some of these relatives remembered her as a young child after coming to America, but then had lost touch with her over the years. She heard more than once, *we always wondered what happened to you. Your parents and Eva when they visited never talked about you. You just disappeared.* Cousins began emailing baby photos of Carrie their own families had preserved. There she was with her two sets of grandparents, one or the other of them holding her in their arms or by the hand. She was usually laughing or grinning in these black and white photos, dressed in lace, ribbons, and beautiful dresses. Again, Carrie was astonished—why did all these relatives have photos of herself as a baby, and why didn't she have any? Actually, she did possess one—she had taken it from one of her mother's albums, a snapshot of herself with her maternal grandmother. Her grandmother's alert and handsome face looked into the camera, holding little Carrie in her broad arms—Carrie herself looked worried, almost yanking at her grandmother's pearl necklace for reassurance. In spite of the anxious look, it still did not seem like the same girl in her elementary and high school photos—that older girl smiled, but there was a forced and insistent, and even manic, quality about those smiles, and that other girl wore plain, dark, unfashionable clothes and a severely-straight bob instead of soft, bouncy curls. *Our grandparents in Malaysia were always fighting over who would take care of you*, one cousin wrote to her, and this was possibly the most surprising and important thing she learned of all.

At the trailhead, a lone bulletin board on oak posts, with a small, attached box of maps, was stationed beneath the shadowy canopy of several aged and cobwebby eucalyptus trees. Push-pinned to the corkboard and protected by a sheet of yellowed, weathered plastic were dozens of old and new flyers: the latest park newsletter on letterhead decorated with a trail of black paw prints, a lemon-yellow brochure warning about rattlesnakes, a turquoise-blue one cautioning about mountain lions and bobcats, a pink calendar of events. Carrie wondered, *whoever even came up this way*? It was a weekend morning, and there was no one around. But someone must have posted the newsletter and calendar fairly recently, some park ranger or volunteer on his way up to the nature center probably. The attached box was full of crisp, freshly-printed maps on green paper. Carrie took one.

The map showed that the North Tamarack Trail was a five-mile loop through what the brochure described as pine forest, sandstone canyon, and coastal sage scrub and chaparral. Carrie meandered along the path for a while, maybe for half a mile, through low, dense thickets of brush. She felt like a giant traversing a miniature forest— the brush came up only to her waist at its tallest. The pale sky remained cloudy, cool, and tranquil overhead. She didn't feel afraid here. True, she always carried her fully-charged cell phone and today she had her pocketknife. It was just that she felt safe in the midst of this low brush, where she could see everything.

During her second visit to Malaysia, her grandparents had moved to a luxurious high-rise in the middle of Lydia. It was very grand and spacious, taking up an entire floor, and overlooking department stores and office buildings. Each morning, her aunt—the wife of the uncle who had inherited everything—took the elevator down to the street corner and bought hot sweetened milk, deep-fried crullers, and fresh vegetables for breakfast. Her grandmother was already very ill with cancer and bedridden at the time. She had lost so much weight, she was little more than a skeleton, very different from the fearsome and magnificent lady of the previous visit. Yet in spite of this, her grandmother wanted to see Carrie and occasionally even tried to press money into her hand, which her mother made her return. *You've always been my favorite*, Grandmother said to her, and back then, Carrie had not understood why. When her mother and aunt were not tending to her grandmother, cooking, or watching soap operas, they ran errands around the city or visited friends and relatives. Carrie tagged along with Eva to the busy marketplaces, where she was both overwhelmed and fascinated by the dumpling shops and crowded open-air stalls, stuffed with piles of clothing, accessories, electronics, toys, and foods of all kinds. One day her family took a taxi up to a mountainside cemetery, to visit her father's family burial grounds. Along the way, they stopped to buy dumplings from a street vendor, whose small cart was perched perilously on the edge of a cliff, framed by the beautiful mountainside and wide blue skies. The cemetery itself was located on a scenic but very steep and rocky area of the mountain. Tombs and memorials of various sizes, some small and modest, others larger and more imposing were scattered among the hills and rocks—

her father's family memorial was among the larger ones, made of marble walls and floors. They paid their respects with candles and fruit, and the silence of the mountains and the wind in the trees seemed to reply. Carrie would always remember the breath-taking and strange beauty of the vast forest spread all around, so deeply green and hushed.

The trail began a gradual upward climb along a sandstone cliff. Clusters of tiny pink and lavender wildflowers poked out among the few patches of dry brush. The cliff looked out over the sage scrub she had just walked through, and far away, she could see silvery flashes of the ocean. Carrie took a sip of water and looked at her watch. It was ten already. Her friend, Nora, had said she might call this morning. Carrie speed dialed Nora's number, but there was no cell reception. She wished she had thought about that before starting her walk—then she could've let Nora know where she was, and they could've planned to talk later.

She had tried to discuss the grandparent situation a few times with Nora, when she visited over spring break. They had eaten lunch together at the food court.

"I wonder how long they were planning to keep it secret," Carrie complained. She had actually not felt very hungry and did not know why she had picked such a gigantic sandwich.

Nora, on the other hand, dug into her salad quite enthusiastically and said, "Yes, that is very weird. A lot of people don't have memories before three or four. Or five."

"I don't remember anything. Nothing at all."

"I don't remember anything before the age of five, myself."

Carrie asked, "What do you think about hypnosis? Maybe I should try it."

Nora's mouth turned down at the sides and her eyes widened.

"I feel like I just found out I had been adopted," Carrie tried again.

"Yes, I can see why you would feel that way," said Nora, "But you don't need to worry. Your parents love you. All parents love their children."

"I don't agree," Carrie said.

"They wanted you back," Nora pointed out.

"My parents said my grandparents couldn't take care of me anymore." Carrie said. No matter how much Carrie argued, Nora adamantly refused to believe any parent could dislike their child.

"Do you remember," Carrie said," when I wrote you that letter back in high school, about how I didn't want to go to school here, but my parents pretended like I had wanted to go."

"Nooo…"

"They kept telling everyone I was the one who had chosen to go here…"

Nora said nothing. Carrie plowed on, "And look at how they paid for Eva to go to…"

"That wasn't fair," Nora had said soothingly, partly because she had heard it all before, and partly because that was the way she was. It was calm and cool Nora, and not Carrie's parents who had kept safe all of Carrie's childhood drawings. She had known Nora since they were both six-years-old, and she sometimes thought of Nora as her "little mom."

Carrie reached the top of the first bluff. She knew the trail would continue upwards again later, but for now, she stopped to look at her damp and crinkled map. She was hot, sweaty, winded, and beginning to feel anxious. The feeling of safety she had felt in the low brush, had completely left her by now. Where was she? She had passed two-mile markers some ways back, but then, the markers seemed to have suddenly all disappeared. The pine forest lay up ahead. It was interesting, with its walls of dark, gnarled trees lining the path and fusing together overhead to form a tunnel, but also a little creepy, like the grabby trees in Snow White.

The wildflowers were sparse here—instead, tall bushes with bright red berries, and shorter bushes of chamise formed a barricade alongside the edges of the canyon. She could see the steep fall of the canyons between the branches, and the regular, more popular trails on the other side of the canyon, like in a faraway painting. A few hikers could be seen on those distant trails, and Carrie suddenly wished she were over on that side. She always seemed to be in the wrong place. But it would take too long to turn around, and she was probably almost to the nature center, anyway. She looked around her one last time—still no one around—and plunged into the woods.

In the tunnel of branches, Carrie felt nervous and watchful; she had never liked enclosed spaces. She knew the tunnel was beautiful, and intellectually she could appreciate its gothic allure, but she wanted to hurry through. A few times, she thought she heard small branches breaking, as if someone were stepping on them or brushing them aside. When she looked behind her, though, she saw nothing, only the sunlight glinting through the leaves. At the end of the tunnel were three shallow naturally formed, granite steps that led back up onto the path. A few feet away, in a clearing, stood the nature center. It was a small, modern-looking glass and wood structure, with large windows looking out over the canyons. She cautiously pushed upon the door— there was no sign indicating she could not do so—and found herself in a small vestibule, opening out into a spacious room, with wall to wall windows. A fire was crackling in a stone fireplace, even though it was warm outside, and then, she noticed all the stuffed animals—a deer, mountain lion, bobcat, owls hanging from the ceiling, squirrels and rabbits and possums, all frozen in action, eternally chasing one another, forever stopping to drink from the glass creek or eyeing stuffed hawks or pelicans or quail hanging from wires or perched upon shelves. There was also a rack of nature books and pamphlets, toys, and T-shirts, a desk by the door, covered with papers, and an empty chair behind the desk; there were several empty benches by the fireplace. No one was in the room.

Disappointed, Carrie sat down on one of the benches, and picked up a book about the Torrey Pines, written by the naturalist and former park ranger, Arthur S. Hayward. The book was small and wire-bound, not a guidebook, but a journal of one person's perspective of the park and its special trees, a leisurely, almost random collection of day to day notes. The cover showed a black and white photo of two young Torrey Pine trees, their trunks still slender and straight, but with the smaller, upper branches beginning to bend into strange shapes. There was also a black and white photo of who she presumed to be a young Arthur Hayward, and he was quite handsome, with dark curly hair, a rakish goatee, black eyes, and ruddy-looking cheeks. He wore hiking pants and boots and a dark button-down shirt, and in the photo, did not seem tall, but looked, in fact, rather impish.

She took out her sandwich and apple and started to read as she ate her lunch. *Juniper plums aren't summer fruit. They aren't made out of juniper and they aren't plums. They aren't even fruit, although if you want to eat one, I think they are supposed to taste pretty good.* On another page: *One day I saw thousands of orange things on the beach. They looked like long, skinny, transparent orange peels with tentacles. "What are those things?" everyone was asking. I found out they were a type of jellyfish called Sea Peraltas. Their tentacles supposedly only give a very mild sting. I didn't get close enough to find out.* And yet on another page: *You can see gray whales migrating from the Bering Sea all the way down to Baja California all along Deacon's Trail, in December or January, swimming by in small groups or sometimes alone.* She turned to another section and read a story about hummingbirds at the zoo, which had little to do with Torrey Pines, but which was still interesting. Finally, at the front of the book, she encountered more familiar territory: *Torrey Pines only grow naturally at Torrey Pines State Reserve.* This she knew already. But he spiraled off onto stories she didn't know: *In 1969, over 50 trees were killed by the heat of a fire, but not one actually burned. The tree, besides adapting to the wind and sandy soil, can also survive fire. Bark beetles, which lay eggs inside the tree trunks, can do more damage when the larvae hatch and feed off the growing tree. The tree fights back by surrounding the larvae in rosin. One beetle can't do much harm, but thousands of them, eating at the insides of the tree can.* Then she read the following: *Torrey Pines have sometimes been mistakenly thought to be the rarest pine tree in the world. They are not. The rarest pine is either the Vietnamese Dalat pine or the Mexican pinon. Although it is the only black pine with seven needles, the Torrey Pine is not the only pine with seven needles. It does not have the largest seed of any pine. It is not the only pine that grows near the ocean. There actually isn't anything terribly unique about the Torrey Pine.* Carrie shut the book. The Torrey Pine was not rare, and not even that unique. That was what Arthur said. She wasn't sure if she like the tone of his voice—as if he were in a perpetual bad mood—but the information was fascinating. And this Arthur—well, he was very good-looking, she had to admit. Even from just this one photo.

A sound outside made her jump—again, like branches snapping. The fire blazed away, and the sun shone outside. She checked her phone—eleven-thirty. She tried dialing out again but there was still no reception. She noticed an exit between two of the large windows overlooking the canyon, and wondered why it was there—also, if maybe that would be a convenient door to leave from instead of the front entrance, as she wasn't too certain if she wanted to see who was walking around outside, following her perhaps.

The door opened easily, and she found herself on the edge of a deep, chaparral-filled canyon. Her gaze was drawn down into the canyon, and she stood mesmerized, thinking how scratchy and pointy-looking the chaparral looked, how uncomfortable it would be to fall down into it. And then, quite unexpectedly the sand and dirt crumbled beneath her feet, her wobbly legs gave way, and she fell, slipping and sliding, tumbling all the way down the side of the canyon.

Carrie felt someone holding her hand. *It's Grandmother,* she thought, although she wasn't sure and couldn't see who it was. It was more of an awareness, or feeling it was her

Grandmother, than anything else. Although it looked and felt like night-time outside, Carrie was not afraid and she walked with whoever it was down a street brightly lit with busy storefronts, strings of globe lights in the trees, the smell of spices and hot noodles and dumplings in the air. In her other hand, Carrie carried a basket full of plums and cookies. These are for Arthur, she told herself, even though, as in all dream-like sequences, she did not know why they were for Arthur or where he was, if he was even alive, or had ever existed. There were people everywhere, but all was silent. Once, she thought she saw her mother's face in the crowd, and then, her father's, Eva's, Nora's, but whenever she tried to look more closely, each one melted away into the other hundreds of faces. Carrie did not feel alarmed at this, only curious. They meant no harm, she knew, and everything would be all right. The sky overhead was a galling purplish-silver hue, backlit by a veiled moon, and up ahead, on the horizon, lay the deeply green and hushed pine forest silhouetted in black.

My little sister was wearing her favorite shirt again, third day in a row—a white Hanes short-sleeve tee, with Electric Woman ironed onto the front. Electric Woman's red boots were peeling off, and the shirt was no longer white, but a patchy tan color. Several drinks may have been spilled and long dried on it.

"Didn't I tell you to put that shirt in the wash?" I said. Suzy stuck her tongue out at me and ran away.

"I'll take you to the zoo if you throw that in the laundry," I called. It was four o'clock and if we left right away, we would have two hours to walk around.

A soft bundled-up something flew into the air and bounced off my shoulder. Suzy was nowhere to be seen, but I could hear something scrambling around in the front coat closet. I smiled and tossed Electric Woman into the washing machine.

Suzy didn't like riding with me, because she always wondered why she had to sit in the back. Her friends apparently were allowed to sit up front.

"I don't have to listen to you," she said, "because you/re not Mom."

To which I replied, "If you don't sit in the back, we're not going." Suzy argued, but I was stubborn. By the time we arrived at the zoo, we were both cranky. I bought us root beer floats, and Suzy stopped whining about being hungry and "scratchy." She was wearing a ruffled white short-sleeve blouse and striped blue skirt—with her brown pigtails and red-framed glasses, she looked like a fancy chipmunk.

We went to see the River Animals first, where a hyperactive river otter scrambled up and down the slippery rocks of a waterfall, jumped up on a hammock, batted around a beach ball, and then, started over again. I felt sorry for the obviously very bored little otter.

A few exhibits away was the tiger. He was out this afternoon, and his orange, white, and black-muscled shoulders rippled as he grabbed and chewed apart a freshly-deceased rabbit. Suzy wanted to leave right away.

Down the hill, an antsy raccoon was pacing back and forth in front of a wire fence. I wasn't sure what a raccoon was doing in a cage next to the Siberian reindeer and Arctic fox, but no matter. Maybe this was a special raccoon. He certainly seemed so, as he suddenly whipped around to stare at me and Suzy. Both black paws gripped the bars of the fence, and his shiny baleful black eyes demanded that we get him out of there, *right now.* I was transfixed by his angry stare until a gawky young boy rushed up with a great deal of (I felt, unwarranted) excitement.

"Mom!" he screamed. "A raccoon! A raccoon! Mom, look! A RACCOON!!" As if this animal were the most unusual one, he had ever seen.

We moved on to the pandas. But even they could not thrill or charm us today. Both Mei Mei and Bao Bao looked out of sorts and cloddish, chewing and breaking branches of bamboo, as if they were unappetizing pretzel sticks.

But the most depressing exhibit of all was a lone gloomy peccary, the saddest animal I had ever seen. He stood in the middle of a cleared space, staring down silently at the ground, immobile, with eyes closed. I felt sorry for the poor guy, and briefly considered breaking down the fence. I could free the peccary—and the otter, hungry tiger, the angry raccoon, and sulky pandas, the whole lot of them. But then what?

"He looks sad," Suzy said. "I want to hug him." We left on this down note. When I asked what she thought of the visit, she replied, "I wish I had worn my Electric Woman T-shirt."

It occurred to me then—I envisioned a light bulb blinking on—that Electric Woman for Suzy was a protector and source of comfort, someone to look up to. Not exactly, as I had imagined before, just someone Suzy wanted to *be* when she grew up—and I regretted my past jabs of, "There is no Electric Woman, Suzy! Get real!" Electric Woman was more of a hopeful vision or possibility.

"I wish I had let you, too," I said. What was more, I wished I had my own Electric Woman T-shirt.

It was forty years ago that she had stood upon this very spot—but in very different circumstances. Forty years ago, there had been no marker here, no walled garden, no willow trees, no rows of birches, or sleeping rose bushes. There had been only rocks, river, sky. The bluff overlooking the river.

There had been a body.

Her mother's body.

They had found her in the river, wearing her heavy winter coat—a belted, gray wool— and her favorite blue dress. But no shoes. They must have floated away, the police said. Or she must have taken them off before falling. Before jumping. (But, shhh, there was no *proof* of that—you cannot say *before jumping*.) It was reported as a fall, a very unfortunate fall. Due to all that alcohol she had consumed. Her mother did not drink, but that day, they found a bottle of Scotch in the front seat of her car parked by the road. Also, a pack of cigarettes, even though she had given up smoking many years earlier.

Her mother had worn her blue-velvet pumps, her favorite pair. This Renee was sure about. The shoes were missing from her mother's closet when she and her Aunt Caroline cleaned it out after the funeral. Mama must've looked pretty that last day, like she used to—long, dark, wavy hair, combed and shiny, wearing her deep-red lipstick and favorite perfume, *White Roses*. After Renee and her mother moved in with Aunt Caroline, Mama had not paid so much attention to her looks. She started to forget things: to go to the hairdressers, to change her clothes, to get out of bed. To eat. She hated seeing her mother growing so thin.

Please, Mama, Renee had said. *Have some soup. It's good for you.*

But her mother had only smiled and shook her head. *No, my darling—I'll eat later. Don't worry about me.*

Except that she never did have something later. Her mother just stopped eating. If she hadn't drowned, she would have probably starved to death.

Her mother's sadness began when Chris, her mother's boyfriend, stopped coming by. This was after they moved in with Auntie. Chris was tall and thin, with blue eyes, a crazy-wide grin, and bright-blonde hair. He was an actor at the Westchester Civic Theater, and had taught Renee how to jitterbug, ice skate, and drive his red T-bird convertible around the block. But Auntie disapproved of Chris, and told him he mustn't come around any longer, he was a bad influence on Renee and Louisa, Renee's mother—he and that entire theater crowd of his. She caught her Aunt whispering things to Chris once, when her mother wasn't around, and then Chris suddenly stopped coming by, didn't even leave a note. Her mother had tried looking for Chris at the Theater, but the following spring, he was gone.

Aunt Caroline was nicer to Mama after Chris left. *He was only after one thing*, Aunt Caroline reminded her. *You're lucky to be rid of him.* She was Mama's older sister, after all, the sensible one in the family—a grade-school principal, also a Sunday School teacher. Auntie was always appropriate, always said the right thing, although it was never original; she never wore anything but the most correct sweater sets, the most sedate black pumps. Yet, there were things about her, too, things that weren't *quite* right. For example, in spite of her stated disdain for gossip, Renee caught her time and time again, talking on the phone (when she did not know Renee was listening), complaining about her mother: how Louisa, little Louisa, had always been the flighty one, the pretty, little, charming thing, the dreamer in the family—and look what good all *that* had been! Louisa couldn't make any money as an actress, couldn't even support her own child. Louisa, while still in high school, had gotten herself into trouble with an older college boy—she was always such a flirt—and he was long-gone by the time baby Renee was born. *Such a resilient child*, Aunt Caroline would whisper over the phone. *I can't believe what she's had to put up with, with all that moving around.*

Renee knew that her aunt wanted her to like her, because she would say things like, *I know you're a good, smart girl. I know all the hard times you've been through,* and

126

she'd give Renee a big smile, offer her homemade cookies, ask her about school—but Annie did not like her. She hated how her aunt's entire being seemed to expand whenever Mama lost another job, when Mama began to lose her looks because she had stopped eating. This though Aunt Caroline would shake her head and sound sympathetic. *It's too bad*, she'd say, *too bad*. And she wouldn't be actually smiling, but it sounded as if she were trying hard not to.

Aunt Caroline got married to her long-time beau, Irwin, and around the time her mother started working part-time as a cashier at the local grocery store—to help out with expenses, she had explained apologetically. Irwin had been impressed with Auntie's generosity and patience in taking in her younger sister and her sister's child.

After Caroline married, Renee began hearing even worse things about Mama around town, especially after she quit her job at the grocery; there were rumors that Mama was lusting after, for godssakes, her ugly, balding Uncle Irwin, her sister's own husband—and after all the generosity Caroline had shown her mother! Renee knew this wasn't true—she saw how Irwin was the one always hanging around Mama, and Mama trying to stay away. Mama got another job at the library. This paid even less than the grocery store, and although Mama seemed happier there, she also stopped eating, became sick more often, had trouble getting out of bed sometimes. Sometimes, when Mama was feeling better in the evenings, the two of them would walk, hand in hand, outside in the garden. Caroline had inherited the house and surrounding acreage from Renee's grandparents. Louisa couldn't be trusted to manage such a large property.

Renee, her mother would say quietly, as they walked in the garden, *you know that I love you. I'm sorry I wasn't a better mother. If I could've just made more money. We could've sailed to a Greek Island, where the sun and the sea are always so blue and beautiful...where everything is beautiful.* Her mother would look at her and smile, that wistful, adoring smile of hers, because her mother thought Renee was beautiful, too. She had told her so, many times.

Aunt Caroline wanted Mama to leave. She needed the spare room for her own baby, which was due in the spring. Perhaps Louisa could stay at a boardinghouse in town? *Renee, of course, can stay here. It won't do for a child to be in a boardinghouse.* But before she was to leave, Louisa had jumped or fallen into the river.

Her mother had a life insurance policy; all the money went to Renee, with a stipulation that she attend a prestigious girl's school in Boston. She never saw her aunt again. This was from choice.

When Renee graduated from university—as valedictorian—and later, become a professor, she bought her her aunt's house, and all the land surrounding it, including the land by the river where her mother died. A garden was planted, and a memorial for her mother. Uncle

Irwin had passed away long ago from cancer, and Caroline was now, alone, in a nursing home. Cousin Jennifer, spoiled, willful, self-centered, was living in Europe with an Italian painter; she rarely flew back to the States. All this, Renee had nothing to do with—except for the house. She had wanted the house and surrounding land, and Jennifer was more than willing to sell the "old farm" in order to live abroad.

While cleaning out a spare bedroom closet one day, she found her mother's blue-velvet shoes. Along with a pack of old letters from Chris, addressed to Mama.

With gloved hands, Renee smoothed the dirt by her mother's grave, over the place where she had buried the willow-wood box holding Mama's shoes and Chris's letters. The sun was setting over the river, its fractured light spreading over the calm, dark water. When Renee threw in the last bag containing her Caroline's things, it made hardly a splash.

Here, it is always late spring, with the long bank of open windows ushering in leafy sunshine and smells of damp soil; the blackboard fills most of the front wall, a world map lies right of that, and rows of smaller maps and art projects—some neat, others not so—travel around the square, white-washed room.

Here, it is always one in the afternoon, where Mrs. Martin, a small, solid woman with glasses and short, wavy hair—still light-brown in late life, a gentle smile, and the quiet of Midwestern farms and grown children, presides over twenty-three developing minds and bodies, all now digesting chicken fried steak, powdered potatoes, preternaturally red apple slices, all now scratching away on sheets of notebook paper bound with handmade covers.

Slowly, up and down the aisles, walks Mrs. Martin, silent, watching. A few heads have already wilted, and rest now upon sweating forearms—some eyes are open, some closed, a few mouths expel soft snores. One by one, the heads droop, and Mrs. Martin walks up and down the aisles.

Mrs. Martin stops and stands next to the girl's desk, smiling. The girl—skinny, dark brown from too much sun, with a home-made haircut and too-short pants—writes and writes and will never look up. She is the only one still writing, hunched over her desk, writing, writing, writing—what day it is, the chicken fried steak-potatoes-apples for lunch, the movie about planets in science class, the sugar-cube pyramid she worked on in social studies. She writes about P.E.—her least favorite class, as she is always next to last to be chosen for teams, before the pale, too-tall, freckled girl. She writes about the birthday party invitation which she hopes she won't have to turn down again. She knows her mother will give her permission this time, she can definitely feel it. She writes about the new song she learned yesterday at piano. But she won't be taking lessons anymore—Mother thinks the piano teacher spends too much time with her (she presses down in thick, dark cursive), and not enough with her older sister. The girl draws three lop-sided stars at the top of the page and shades them in with a yellow colored pencil. It was a good day, she writes. That's what three stars mean.

The girl looks up, with hopeful eyes, looks up at Mrs. Martin, who is always there, quiet, smiling, always speaking to her in kind, approving tones—and gladness and wonder, but also small violets of pain sink tiny roots into the girl's heart, tendrils that stretch and multiply with each passing day.

They have five minutes. Number Seven skips the small talk. What do you do? What do you do for fun? What's your favorite sport? Cleft chin, light-colored eyes. Expensive-looking shirt. Aggressive smile.

Next.

Number Eight. Brown hair, dark eyes. T-shirt, jeans. Tanned, surfs, owns gardening company. Checks out girl at opposite table.

Next.

Bookish, glasses, likes classical music. Frowns when she says she likes author, Z—. Next. Tallish, polo shirt, receding hairline, eyes, nose, mouth, asks: What sign are you?

Number Eleven. Hair, eyes, nose, mole near mouth. Traveled the world. Little eye contact. Next, next, next. Names, information, faces blur. She considers moving to mountains to contemplate trees and sky for rest of life.

Number Thirty, Number Forty, Number Fifty. Sixty. Something's wrong here. Medium height, dark hair. A blank face? Yes, an oval disc with no features. No eyes, no nose, no mouth. How does he breathe, talk? She looks away, down at square, brown hands, clean nails, a pinky ring with an unusual blue stone. Perfectly fitting shirt in a slate color. Silver cufflinks. Pleasant voice issues forth from blank being. Forty-one, financial management, divorced, classics background, reads Ancient Greek history in spare time. She counts to ten, looks back at face. Relieved to see features now reappearing. Square face, brown eyes, crooked nose, smiling mouth. When the buzzer rings—after puddle-faced Number One Hundred—she has ten numbers written down, but remembers only Number Sixty, with the blue ring.

The one she had blanked out on, but then, thought was rather handsome.

THE MAN WITH THE
CARTIER WATCH

Twenty-four-year-old Julia Cross had acquired over the years an increasing and uneasy fascination with the occult, with the supernatural, with the mysteries and coincidences of life—and most especially, with psychics. There was something irresistible, Julia imagined, about having someone answer all the complex questions of life without having to divulge, on her end, any personal information, or even having to establish any sort of committed relationship. You need only pay this special person a certain amount of money, and he or she would reveal everything, unlock the secrets of your life, or at the very least, predict what was in store and help you along your way. For surely someone must know all these things—she had always been one to believe in reasons and answers. And this was how Julia found herself seated one late October morning, in the dim, incense-scented kitchen of the world-famous psychic, Jonathon Todd. Todd had read the palms of rock stars and royalty—yes, indeed, he was not called the Psychic to the Stars for nothing, and how she ever was able to schedule an appointment with him was something beyond her wildest imaginings. Julia had found out all about Jonathon Todd from a women's magazine, and now here she was—just for fun, she had told herself—face-to-face with the rumpled-looking, bookish, although not unfashionable, psychic-star himself, nervously looking on as he expertly shuffled a very worn, very yellowed pack of tarot cards. Todd had owlish, alert, brown eyes, magnified by black-rimmed, round glasses, and his hands were plump and soft-looking. As he cut and flipped down the cards, he talked fast, impatiently, and she almost expected him to start snapping his pudgy fingers along with his predictions.

"One of your parents just had an operation," he said. "Your dad I think. He's recovering well, although it'll be a while before he's up and running again."

Julia nodded politely, disappointed that she did not feel more overwhelmed by surprise; her father, indeed, had a bypass done over the summer—or at least that's what she had heard from her sister, Annie. She hadn't talked to her parents in five years.

"You're not close to your parents," Todd continued eerily, "though they would like to be closer. You can visit and all that, but it'd be best to keep your distance." Then he looked over at her carefully, as if seeing something abnormal or even dangerous in her face. Maybe he was just confirming if he was right, although it wasn't that kind of look at all. He sounded too sure of himself.

"I've kept my distance all right," said Julia, sitting up a little now. "I haven't talked to them for a long time. And I don't plan on visiting."

Todd nodded and went on, "You're not married, don't have a boyfriend right now..."

Here, Julia felt compelled to blurt out, "I do have a boyfriend!"

"Well, I don't see him."

"What do you mean you don't *see* him?"

"You look like you're alone."

She opened her mouth to speak and then shut it—must be careful, she thought, she had already talked too much. But before she could stop herself, she heard her voice, low and uncertain, "So he's not the one?"

Todd shook his head decisively. "He's not the one." He was studying her again.

"You know," he said, "you're just not good at picking out men. In an entire room of men, you'd pick the worst one."

"Oh, really?" was all she could manage in her surprise. She suddenly envisioned tall, athletic Jeff standing in a police line-up, with puppy-dog eyes, holding up a placard that read, "Pick Me. I'm the Worst."

"Get rid of him. Them. And look for someone new. Someone you can look up to, someone people will say, 'God, she's lucky to be with that guy.' You know, the man with the Cartier watch."

The man with the Cartier watch—that had a definite ring to it. Well, it was true that Jeff, her boyfriend, was not the Cartier watch type. He was the no-watch type. He carried around one key in his jeans pocket and wore black

T-shirts. Yes, catchy phrase, that—the man with the Cartier watch. Now she wouldn't be able to get it out of her head. She would probably start looking for guys with Cartier watches. Whatever Cartier watches looked like. She had no idea. She herself owned a Timex.

"Don't worry, there will be others," assured Todd briskly, and he began shuffling the cards and slapping them down on the table again. "Now. Are there any specific questions you'd like to ask?"

"Actually, I'd like to hear about my career."

"Good, good. Your career." Todd cheered up. "You're doing some sort of office work now. Is that right?"

"Yes, I work at a non-profit."

"But it's not really what you want to do. You need something much more...much more creative. More glamorous. Like TV. Or film production. Something to do with TV or film."

"Really?"

"Yeah, yeah. You should take up any opportunity to do TV or film work that you can."

"Wow." Julia was genuinely shocked. She had never considered anything remotely similar. And she thought she had tried everything.

"But you shouldn't be in front of a camera. Definitely not. You should do something behind the scenes."

She was beginning to not like this Jonathon Todd. She wondered if there was something wrong with her clothes or make-up, or maybe it was her expression—someone had once told her she looked too serious, like an accountant, and Julia could see how that would not be exactly movie-star material. Still, she wasn't that bad looking—not too short, not too tall, not too thin, not too fat, with so-so, light-brown hair, and attentive, hazel eyes (her best feature, she thought)—and she wondered again why he had looked at her so strangely. But never mind, she told herself, this was all distraction. TV and film were not at all what she wanted to do. There was only one thing she had ever really wanted to be.

"I was wondering," she ventured. "I've always wanted to be…will I ever be…" She sighed, took a breath, and gasped out, "An artist? A painter? An illustrator, maybe?"

Todd looked at her steadily for a few seconds, and then said, "No."

———

Julia was glad that Jeff was away for the week. His older brother, Ben, was moving to a new apartment, and Jeff had driven to Baltimore to help him out. That was typical of Jeff—anyone who needed help, he would. She used to like that about him, except now she realized he pretty much helped anyone, and not just those close to him. This sounded good, but it meant he was always off helping someone or other, and she would find herself spending another weekend alone.

He had left Saturday, and would not be home until the following Friday, and she was relieved by the wide expanse of time stretching ahead of her. She would need it to think about the disturbing things the psychic had said. She had not been expecting such contrary and infuriating advice—psychics were supposed to tell you positive and encouraging things, weren't they? What did they really know? And who was this Jonathon Todd anyway! She couldn't quite bring herself to call him a fraud—he had looked so well-fed and affluent and respectable. But a fraud was probably what he was. *He was trying to help you*, a nasty little voice piped up inside her head. Granted, she could see how "doing something in TV and film" would sound glamorous to many, but they sparked nothing—absolutely nothing—in Julia. Was there something wrong with her? She wished she could to talk to someone about it, *right now*, but she didn't dare call Annie, who would give her a two-hour lecture, and her friend, Dana, was away for the weekend, visiting her own parents. As for Jeff—well, even if Jeff had been home, she would not have told him about the psychic. Not right away, at least. Jeff was surprisingly superstitious, especially for an engineer, and would have probably made things worse, by not treating the whole incident with complete contempt. She would've appreciated disgusted laughter thrown at her, but he would not have laughed. So that day, after the psychic's unwelcome revelations, she kept herself busy, just to give herself things to do and time for her rattled feelings to settle—she ran every errand she could think of, including washing and vacuuming her car and replacing her cell phone battery. She took a walk at the park, and then treated herself to a leisurely manicure and pedicure. Then, feeling a little sorry for herself, she ate dinner alone at her favorite restaurant, Golden East. This was a small, drab-looking place, outfitted with only a few rickety tables and cramped booths, but the food was tasty and inexpensive, and it was located in a busy shopping plaza, right next to her favorite used bookstore. She went into the bookstore after dinner, browsed awhile, and purchased a dictionary-sized volume of Art Deco painters.

Finally, she had to go home, which was a tiny apartment she and Jeff now shared, located six blocks south off of Lexington Avenue. She set down her art book on a side table and turned on all the lights, every single one of them, even the tiny, piano lamp. The room was small and comfortable, but cluttered, with walls of books, the old piano, the lamps, a yellow sofa, silk curtains, a wool rug upon the wood floor. She switched on the television, and the screen flickered on—a news channel. There was the sound of talking. She sat on the floor, because it seemed safer there, on the ground, and watched the flickering blue screen, while the anchorwoman talked and smiled and laughed with her co-anchors. After some time, Julia remembered she had wanted coffee, but she didn't feel like moving. She wanted to sit and do nothing. Her shoes were beginning to hurt her feet, but she kept them on, in a kind of triumphant, passive defiance. A not unpleasant feeling of satiety began to ooze into her consciousness, as if she had been in a struggle, and could now relax and let down her guard. She could try to be normal—work her nine to five job, watch television in the evenings, go to the movies on the weekends with Jeff, go to lunches with her friends, do a little painting and drawing on the side, when she had time. She would join some kind of club or pick up a new hobby, make new friends, and hang out with them, wherever people hung out. This might all work out—she would be too busy, pursuing a balanced life, to go to art school. She remembered something she had heard on the radio the other day. The talk show host had said that the number one reason people did not more diligently pursue their deepest interests, during their spare time, was because they were tired. And I am so very tired, thought Julia. Why can't I be tired like everyone else? She heard the psychic's voice again, unwelcome and fascinating. Where had she heard that voice before? *Find the man with the Cartier watch. You will never be an artist, anyway. You will never be an artist. You will never be anything.* No, she corrected, he hadn't said that. That was from some other time.

From a much longer time ago.

———

"I can't believe he said that!" said Dana, when they finally were able to get together on Monday. Dana was short, heavyset and excitable, with glasses, freckles, and bobbed, frizzy, blonde hair, while Julia was taller, skinnier, and more shy, with long, straight, brown hair. They were a pair in contrasts, and Julia definitely appreciated that. She wasn't sure she would have liked having a close friend exactly like herself. That would've driven her nuts, to be around someone else just as indecisive, blathering, and anxious as she was. *Well, what about your good points*, she felt obligated to argue with herself. *Probably, she would have been jealous of the friend having exactly the same talents that she had*, she answered. *You just can't win,* she scolded herself.

On this dreary, gray Monday, she and Dana were on their lunch hour for an emergency meeting. Julia had just related the details of her psychic visit.

"He was way off!" said Dana, poking critically through a pile of shriveled chicken parts at the food bar. "And give me a break with that 'you'll never be an artist' business!"

"I know. I could have gone to my parents to hear that."

"And that part of you being alone—you and Jeff have been together forever. You're like an old, married couple."

"Well, maybe he meant, that I had this look of being spiritually alone."

"That's what those people would like you to think. Saying stuff that could be interpreted a million different ways."

"He did get the part about my parents right."

"Most people do have surgeries at some point in their lives."

"No, I mean the part about not being close to them."

"Well, maybe you just have this very self-sufficient look. I don't think that proves he's psychic or anything. They just know how to read people! He could tell just by looking at you."

"What could he tell?"

"That you weren't happy. Why aren't you getting anything to eat?"

Quickly, Julia grabbed a plate, and speared a flabby slice of watermelon. "So I don't look happy?" she asked, but Dana was already leaving for their table.

"I'm happy," she informed the top of Dana's head.

"Okay."

"Why do you think I'm not happy?'

"Because you don't look happy."

"That's because of the psychic! I was perfectly happy until I met him. I can't believe I paid two hundred dollars to be told to give up the two most important things in my life."

"Well, they just make things up. Why did you need to ask him anyway? You're great at drawing. You've had sketches published. You even sold one."

"That was when I was ten,"

"And remember that time when you won first place in that art contest? So he's wrong, that's all. As for Jeff, I don't think he's going anywhere. The point is this—what do you see in him?" Julia was always mystified when people asked this.

"We have so many things in common. And he's gorgeous. Don't you think so?"

"He's a normal guy," said Dana carefully. "Average. Normal."

"But he's so intelligent..."

Silence.

"The pasta is terrible today," said Julia, a petulant whine beginning to creep in pitch and volume. "Tastes like—I don't know—mush or something."

"I'm sorry, I should have chosen a better place to eat. I've gotten so used to coming here."

Dana patted her hand, sighing. "Aw, I'm sorry. I'm being horrible today. Don't worry. And hey, I know a great pizza place not far from here and I'll take you next time. It just seems I never see you much anymore." Julia knew she wanted to add "after you moved in with Jeff" but she had thankfully left that out.

They ate in silence, and then Dana pointed out the window. "Look. Isn't that your boss?"

Julia saw the short, powerful, purposeful figure of her supervisor, Howard Nielson, striding into the deli next door, probably to pick up a sandwich to take back to the office with him. He always lunched at his desk and disapproved of anyone else who did otherwise.

"Yeah, that's him. I'm surprised he didn't bring his lunch."

"And so how's your job going?"

"Okay. We're getting ready for a conference so things are a bit hectic right now."

"Has Howard been any nicer to you?"

Julia thought a moment, and realized with surprise that he hadn't. "No, he's still being a snob about the entire Ph.D. thing." Countless times she had complained to Dana about Howard's Ph.D. hang-up—she, Julia, was not as educated as Howard (or as Nancy or Jane or the other PhDs in the office, for that matter), and so therefore could not possibly be as smart or important. She, Julia, held only a Bachelor's, so she did not deserve to have the same privileges as he or the others, such as leaving the office for lunch or having flex hours. But this kind of talk was getting entirely too boring for Julia—and for Dana as well, she was sure.

"What's going on with you?" she asked her friend, hoping to change to a more interesting topic. But Dana didn't seem to have much to report, either.

"Absolutely nothing. I'm teaching at Woodside High School next year, instead of at the middle-school—but I'll tell you about that some other time." She put a hand on Julia's arm. "Don't let that psychic get to you. You know you can do it. Go to art school again. Or don't go to art school and just paint!"

"I can't."

"Why not?"

"I don't have the money."

"Does it take that much money? You already have supplies. And as for school, you can take out a loan. Or get a scholarship! You can go to night school!"

Julia was silent for a moment, taken aback by her friend's unexpected enthusiasm. She hadn't known Dana had felt so strongly about her painting—or how much she hated psychics.

"Okay," she said, finally. "I'll think about it."

―――

Back at the office, Julia checked her voicemail, then her email, and then got down to work preparing mailing labels for the conference invitations. An hour later she had forgotten all about the psychic and Jeff and Dana, and was fighting to stay awake. It was hot in the office—the air conditioning wasn't working again—and she felt dizzy and nauseated. There were still three more hours to go. And where was everyone? She put her chin in her left hand, trying to think of which area she should tackle, and started doodling upon the large calendar that covered almost her entire desk—the paper was clean and white and unmarked, because it was still the beginning of the month and she had not yet written in any of the researchers' schedules. Howard walked in just then from the conference room, which also served as the library, and she hurriedly put a stack of mailing labels on top of her drawing.

"Could you enter these into the database today?" he said, throwing down a stack of journals with their pages marked, onto her desk. He looked particularly repulsive today, with sweat-stains showing on his wrinkled blue shirt, and crumbs stuck like lint pills on his mismatched brown pants. He had a fat, pale face and thick white fingers. Sometimes he looked positively vampiric, but not in a good way—cold eyes and red mouth, oily black hair. Still he was intelligent and persevering. At the age of forty-three, he had a Doctorate in Education and had already published three books and fifteen articles.

"Sure," answered Julia politely. "But Nancy also asked that I finish mailing out the brochures this afternoon, so I might not be able to get them all in until tomorrow."

Pink splotches, like ominous carnations, bloomed suddenly upon Howard's face. "You had plenty of time this morning to get those mailed out. Were you working on something else?"

"Just some filing," stammered Julia. "The copy place didn't have the brochures ready until ten so I couldn't really do anything with them until then."

"You said these brochures would be mailed out before lunch! I didn't see you in here for half the morning."

"I had to go out for stamps," said Julia, trying to keep her voice from quavering. "Also, I just got back from lunch. I did tell Nancy about the brochures being dropped off late. She said it was okay to get them out by five."

"I am your supervisor and not Nancy," shouted Howard, the patches on his face deepening to an even uglier and more alarming crimson. "And you get these done first and mail out the brochures afterwards." He glared at her and stalked out of the office. Julia felt tears collecting in her eyes, and willed them not to drip down her face. They did anyway. She was angry with herself for behaving so childishly. Get yelled at a little and here she was falling apart. Howard didn't have any right to talk to her like that though. Why was she putting up with this? She was actually ahead of schedule on the brochures, because she had used some new software to do all the formatting. Howard hadn't liked it when she had first suggested the software, but she had gone ahead and purchased it anyway, with Nancy's permission. Was that why he was so upset? And Nancy was one of her supervisors—hadn't she been hired to assist all of the researchers? Howard had trained her, but Nancy had hired her. There must be something else—she tried to think of what but her head was pounding, it was so hot, and she felt her lunch traveling back up from where it had been sluggishly digesting. She was going to throw up this minute if she didn't get out of there. But she stayed rooted to her seat, paralyzed by something which would not allow her leave, would not even let her get up from her chair. *Get back to work,* she said to herself. *Don't be such a child.* Yet she could not touch the keys of her computer. She sat there for several minutes, staring at her computer, which was turned off, blankly reflecting back her blank face. Finally, with what seemed like the most gigantic effort, she stood up and walked towards Nancy's office. The door was partially open and Nancy was reading papers at her desk, looking clean, crisp, and efficient as usual, with her perfectly-ironed white blouse and short, neat, bobbed haircut. Nancy was the most meticulous and critical of all the researchers and for this reason, Julia often felt uncomfortable and grubby in her presence. But Nancy also had the calmest personality, so Julia liked her best.

"Are you okay?" said Nancy. She obviously hadn't heard Howard's outburst.

Julia shook her head. "I'm not feeling well. I had an argument with Howard. I need to go home."

Nancy, who didn't like Howard either, merely replied, "Call me when you feel better."

Julia turned to go, but then remembered, "By the way, the brochures are almost all done. I'll mail out the ones I've finished."

"Don't worry about it."

Julia nodded but felt such a surge of guilt that she almost changed her mind, and said she would stay. But then she remembered that Howard would be coming back soon—wherever he was—and the thought of seeing him again was unbearable.

———

It was still early afternoon when she left and there were few passengers on the train. She was able to find a completely empty car—it was so wonderful to pick and choose among the many empty seats rather than cramming in with hundreds of other hot, sweating bodies. Often there were no available seats when she rode back at night and she had to stand, packed in between exhausted-looking men in wrinkled trench-coats and preoccupied women in ill-fitting suits, trying not to breathe in the smell of cheap scent covering up the older, denser odor of unwashed bodies. Julia sat in the back, next to a broad window, and took out a black, wire-bound notebook from her bag. She had dozens of others like it at home, filled with drawings. As the train lurched off to a start and glided out of the station, she gazed dreamily out the window, pencil in hand, blank paper on her lap. The day had transformed from an unpromising, nondescript morning into an unusually pleasant afternoon, with mild, fall sunlight flooding in generously upon the bright-orange seats, with the train so peaceful and empty, with almost a whole day still in front of her, with the detested office behind her. She no longer felt sick and dizzy, but was energized, as if all her anxiety had drained out of her—seeped away, perhaps, into the cracks of the hard, worn sidewalks she had left behind. What if she never went back again? Just called in and quit? The idea appalled and fascinated her. There were people who did that, lots of them probably, but she had never been one of them. She had always been too conscientious—not a day late for work in her life, not one sick day, even during that March blizzard last year. But what could possibly happen, could be so horrible if she just quit? For one, it wasn't like quitting her art class, like she had done years ago—this seemed different somehow. Certainly she would feel awful for not fulfilling her contract with Nancy, her promise to stay for the long-term. But that was before she had known what Howard was really like. Anyway—what could they really do? They would be mad. Okay, she could probably handle that. She was pretty sure they wouldn't sue her or stalk her or do anything violent. Would she even miss anything about the job? It paid well, she liked working with Nancy (with everyone besides Howard, actually), and she even enjoyed the easy, busy mindlessness of it at times. But now come to think of it, that all counted for very little, compared to what she could be doing. Compared to a day like this, where she could be free and doing what she liked—and perhaps, making a little money while she was at it. She tried to imagine what it would be like if she could just draw all day, and she found that idea so enticing, it frightened her, and she immediately pushed it back out of her mind. But she considered it, cautiously, again—of course, lots of people worked at jobs they loved. Everyone except her parents. Both had seemingly disliked their jobs—her father as a doctor, her mother as a teacher—because they were always complaining about work. They always talked about money and security and retirement. They had taught her that true happiness lay in some mystical afterlife. *You won't make any money as an artist*, they had said. *You can do that kind of thing after you retire.* Their voices spoke to her, on and on, as usual, becoming more and more sneering, when she tried to argue back: *No one will buy your work. You're not good enough. Blah, blah, blah.* She always listened.

Julia sighed, settled back on the seat, and idly started sketching an anonymous profile—one eyebrow, eyelashes, half a mouth, one eye. She often started out drawings like this, when she had no subject in mind. It was automatic, and the motions allowed her to relax and think. She could not give up drawing; there was no doubt in her mind about this. But the psychic's predictions had upset her, more than she would have ever expected. He was, as Dana had pointed, just a total stranger who knew how to read people—and he wasn't even very accurate. He told me I can't be an artist, Julia finally concluded, just because I don't look like one.

———

Jeff came home on Saturday morning, and not Friday.

"Now be reasonable," he sighed over breakfast at a nearby diner—its convenient location near their apartment was its biggest attraction. "Don't give up your job. It's the best paying one you've ever had."

"I just can't work there. Howard hates me for some reason and I can't work for someone...in an environment like that. Most of my projects are with him." She took another sip of orange juice—she felt like celebrating this morning, but unfortunately, Jeff wasn't cooperating. She didn't blame him—without her income, they would now have to be more careful with expenses.

"There are people like Howard everywhere. I deal with difficult people all the time. You just have to find a way to get along with him."

"What if I don't want to?"

"Let me guess. Did Dana talk you into this?"

"No, she didn't. Although she agreed with me. And I'm going to take art classes again."

Jeff swallowed a bit of pancake, as if it were a block of wood, and tried to look pleasantly supportive. "Okay. That's great. But aren't those classes expensive?"

"I can take out student loans, get part-time work, whatever. I was thinking of maybe applying for a job at a museum or art store."

They both picked at their still-full plates unenthusiastically. He was having the Farmer's Breakfast and Julia had ordered scrambled eggs and toast. The eggs on her plate looked overly solid and brownish, like they had been overcooked, rather than soft and creamy as she preferred them. She ate most of it anyway.

"It's just that I hate to see you leave because of Howard," said Jeff. "You're letting him win."

"Win what? As I see it, it is he who is losing a good worker. I can always find another job."

"Did you tell Nancy about the problems with Howard? You couldn't work for someone else in the company?"

"No, Jeff. You know I've tried everything," she said patiently. "Listen, I've thought this over, and I am not changing my mind. I just refuse to work for someone as moody and difficult as Howard." She suddenly reached over and held his hands in hers. "Why do we have to be like this anyway? We'll be all right. And shouldn't we be supportive of each other instead of always fighting?"

Jeff enunciated precisely, "We aren't fighting," and then he smiled. "Anyway. Wouldn't it be boring if we agreed about everything? I like it when people have different views from myself. I don't want to be around a bunch of sycophants."

"Just because people agree on the same things doesn't mean they're sycophants!"

"You know what I mean," he smiled.

"Why can't you ever be on my side," she began.

"But I am on your side," said Jeff, surprised. "You know, you're acting really strange tonight. Are you okay? You know I just want what's best for us. For you."

Julia contemplated him across the table. He seemed to be saying the right things, but he didn't look right. He seemed strangely smaller than usual, his eyes closer together, and his obediently spiky, gelled hair, which she normally found cute, now annoyed her. "You're right. I don't think he's really psychic or whatever. Maybe he's just perceptive. Maybe he's even right about some things."

When he asked, like what, she just shook her head and went on holding his hand. He smiled at her, and started talking about moving to a better place, a bigger apartment. The familiar woozy feeling drifted back into her consciousness, a rush of momentary relief. But the psychic's words echoed in her mind—*he's not the one, the man with the Cartier watch*—and she knew now that it was too late, that the psychic's voice would be there a long time. And she knew, at the core of her heart, even if there were such a one as the Man with the Cartier Watch, she would probably not want him. The fortune-teller's voice would merely join the cacophony of familiar voices already crowded in her head— those harsh voices from the past, the accusing voices from the present—but growing ever fainter, fainter, and fainter as each long year passed.

Nina was outraged.

"I *told* her!" she shouted, grabbing fistfuls of her hair, "I wanted a layered bob with *bangs!* And look, look, *look* at this! What *is* this!"

"It looks all right to me," said her little sister, Kathie. "It's just…different."

Nina hissed, "It's a *mullet*, for god sakes! A mullet!"

To reinforce the awfulness, Nina googled *mullet* on her laptop, and was bombarded by a dozen photos of shirtless, tattooed, overweight men, sporting long, curly hairdos with short bangs and short sides—sort of like Nina's cut. Kathie giggled.

"Now I have to drive all the way to San Diego to *fix* this," fumed Nina. Her former stylist, Rachelle, was in San Diego. It would be a good hour's drive. This was what she got for sashaying into a place called Cheap Cuts. As if any old place would do.

Rachelle was also an aesthetician and had been after Nina for some time to do the permanent make-up thing. *You won't have to apply that black eye-liner every day anymore*, insisted Rachelle. *Or the eyebrow pencil. I promise, you'll love it.*

Nina always said no, but today, she wavered. Not once had Rachelle messed up on her hair. And she had fixed her mullet, sort of—chopped off the back part so that it now looked like a very short bob.

For moral support, Rachelle took Nina around the salon to look at all the other women who had had the procedures done on them. Nina was surprised that there were so many. The women looked normal—just women wearing make-up. Most of them older than Nina. They gently but firmly encouraged Nina to do the procedures. It seemed very important that Nina do the procedures.

So, Nina, drawn into this sea of soft, feminine approval, of caresses and smiles, succumbed and let Rachelle do the eyeliner and brows. It would save so much time, and she would always look good.

It won't hurt, Rachelle promised.

But it did hurt. It hurt like hell.

A girl, staring at Nina's Goth-black eyeliner and brows as she walked out of the salon, said, "Oh that's so pretty!" But Nina did not feel pretty. She felt numb.

At home, Kathie avoided comment.

"I know it's awful," said Nina.

Later that night, while staring at her black-rimmed eyes, her thickly-penciled, black brows in the mirror, she said to Kathie, "I miss my old face."

"Doesn't that stuff ever wear off?"

"Rachelle said it would, but I read otherwise on the internet."

"I guess that's why it's called permanent make-up…," Kathie stopped. "I'm sure it really will wear off, Nina."

Nina sat down on her bed, stunned. "Ohmigod. I don't want to look like this all the time." She realized—too late—that she had *liked* having different looks. The changeability of her old face.

Now she had only this face. This carved-on, glamorous—this hateful—new face.

Kathie said, "Well, at least, your hair will grow out."

MULTITUDES

November in Northern Virginia. The time of year Anne liked best, at least in that part of the world, and from her daughter's living room window, she admired the red, gold, and copper colored leaves, falling silently from the tall trees, usually a few at time, but sometimes, when a sudden gust of wind blew through, in a much greater quantity—and then it seemed as if it were raining leaves, adding to the deep, brown, rustling sea already blanketing the lawn. The gentle morning sun was shining through the branches and the only sound throughout the house was the tiny, meticulous tickings of the porcelain clock on the fireplace mantelpiece.

Technically, Anne was on vacation for the next few weeks—it helped that the office was three thousand miles away—and she could relax and dream a little, grudgingly admitting to herself that she was glad Roxanne and Richard, her son-in-law, had chosen this house in Great Falls. Anne only visited at Thanksgiving and sometimes during the summer, a pleasant change from her condo in California. She liked to imagine this place, cut off from the rest of the world, self-contained, apart from the noise and business, people and troubles, which lay only a few miles away. This would have been the kind of place, she thought, she would

have liked to have grown up in – silent, spacious, isolated—
the kind of home she wished she had provided for Roxy.
Instead, Roxy had grown up in a cramped, one-bedroom
condo in San Diego, while Anne had worked long hours at
various jobs—as a waitress, temp, office assistant, and
finally, as an office manager. Roxy's father, Jeff, had left
when Roxy was two, but Anne did not want to think of that.
Remembering only brought back pain and anger—Jeff had
left Anne for one of his co-workers, a fellow teacher and a
former friend of hers. Because of this, Anne had found
herself trusting people less and less over the years, losing
interest in those around her, losing contact even with her
own relatives, choosing instead to focus on work and raising
Roxy; it had been a gloomy, and yet sometimes satisfying
self-sufficiency, with just the two of them. In San Diego,
they had been able to build a stable life—Anne's work,
Roxy's school, Roxy's art and music lessons, the same stores,
the same restaurants, the same neighbors, the same politely
friendly circle of co-workers, friends, and acquaintances. It
wasn't perfect. It wasn't exciting. But it was better than what
Anne had had in her own early childhood, shuttled around
from relative to relative, all over the country.

Now, all the hard times were past, it seemed, and little
Rachel, Anne's four-year-old granddaughter, would live
here, in this big house, and enjoy an ideal childhood. Roxy
was happy here, with her new studio, the house, and of
course, with Richard, a promising young research scientist.

160

For years, Roxy had tried to convince her mother to move to the area—California was so far away, Thanksgiving and summer visits were not enough, and didn't Anne want to be near everyone anyway? It was true, Roxy and Richard and Rachel, were indeed "everyone" in Anne's life—she liked to joke that they were the three necessary Rs in her life. But as to other people, the walls she had built around herself over the years had done well in keeping them out, or at least at a safe distance.

Now, without Roxy around, Anne was lonely. She couldn't deny this. But to move, back to this part of the world and away from all that was solid and comfortable in San Diego—that she didn't think she could do. What was more, this was Virginia, and Virginia was The South, and Anne did not want to live anywhere near the South. Some of it was because of the stories she had heard from friends about the South, maybe some of it was stories she herself had read about in the papers and books, and maybe some of it was from her own visits to the area—the Confederate flag that she had seen hanging in front of a house in Alexandria, the perceived snubs at the stores; from all this, perhaps, she had formulated her stubborn, inexorable dislike of the area. All of these things were reasons—but there was more. Anne had spent a few years in South Carolina with her Aunt Doreen as a young child, and those years had been among the worst in her life. Her Aunt Doreen had been cruel, and there had been bullying at the school she had attended. She had been called a colorful variety of names and the worst was not knowing enough about her own background to deny the accusations – so she denied them all. She was aware, of course, that she didn't look like the other kids—anyone could see that—but then she didn't look like any of her relatives either. Anne's mother had been a wild one, running off with some mysterious boyfriend, and then living in a commune, before finally being dragged back by her parents—by then, she was pregnant with Anne, the boyfriend was long gone, and she was dying from cancer. She never revealed who Anne's father was. Anne could not remember her mother, and no one felt it necessary, or wise, to answer her questions. There had never even been any photos of Anne's mother, although she had heard that she was once beautiful. On the other hand, there had been plenty of speculation about Anne's father—who he might be, where he might be, if he was in jail or lying dead in the proverbial ditch—none of it ever certain. All that she knew was that she did not look like her mother, nor anyone on her mother's side. Her hair was light-brown and curly, rather than black and straight; her skin was smooth and brown, like caramel, rather than fine and white, like china; her eyes were black and almond-shaped, and not large and deep-set and green or hazel; she was small and wiry, rather than tall and big-boned. Her looks were always a source of comment, and she was glad that Roxy had inherited Jeff's good looks, rather than her own mixed features.

On Anne's first day of grade school in Fresno, California—where she eventually went to live with an aunt and uncle after the aunt in South Carolina suddenly died—the teachers had asked the children to form a circle and introduce themselves. When it was Anne's turn, someone asked, are you Mexican? Anne answered, no, which started off a persistent round of questioning. Are you Indian? Are you Italian? Chinese? Japanese? Australian? French? African? South American? And so forth, all to which Anne quite calmly answered no. When all the countries of the world, it seemed, had been exhausted, the children, and the teachers for that matter, sat in silent perplexity, and finally admitted that they had given up – and so what was she, anyway? To which Anne had triumphantly replied, "American!" She was surprised it had taken them so long to say it. And the children had sighed in relief or disappointment, but glad, mostly, to have the mystery solved, more or less. Anne had gone home that day and told her aunt and uncle what had happened. Why hadn't the kids been able to figure out what she was? Her aunt and uncle had looked at each other, and her aunt, a quiet and calm woman, already nearing her sixties at the time, told Anne that she had said the right thing. Anne was grateful for that; South Carolina was not such a hurtful time anymore. It was in the past. It was far away.

On the mantelpiece, the porcelain clock chimed ten. Time to go. She hopped off the window seat, pulled on her long, winter socks, her boots, her red jacket. Picked up her keys, a manila folder, and her purse from the foyer table, opened the front door, and stepped out into a rain of falling leaves and cold autumn sunshine.

She was to pick up Rachel at the Montessori school at twelve, as Roxy was in Washington D.C. this morning— Anne had insisted that she take some time off, and so Roxy had chosen to spend a day at the Smithsonian, taking in a lecture at the art gallery and meeting with some friends for lunch. Secretly, Anne had planned to look at a few properties in the area, before picking Rachel up, just to see what was available. The real estate agent she had half-heartedly been working with couldn't meet this morning, so Anne decided to do a few drive-bys of her own. The houses she had selected were all carefully mapped out, with directions, in her folder, and she was trying to read these (even though she had it all practically memorized in her head), while also trying to keep her eyes on the road. She hated driving here, as everyone always seemed to be in such a hurry, even more so than in San Diego. As if to emphasize this, a driver in a battered, black sedan honked at her, and then zoomed past along the shoulder of the road, apparently because she had refused to make her left turn directly into oncoming traffic, so that he could pass.

"I can't believe it," she muttered, "I should get killed just so you can drive by a split second faster, is that it?" She was already nervous, and now she was also in a bad mood. Still, she resolved not to let the other driver rattle her, because she couldn't be late to pick up Rachel. She worried about driving too fast, and then getting pulled over by some bored policeman, or maybe—she didn't even want to think about this—she'd even get a flat tire. Why not just forget this whole thing, she told herself, and wait for the agent to do the driving. Why not just forget about looking at houses. She didn't want to live here. She could just drive to a Starbucks, right now, and treat herself to a tall vanilla latte, instead of submitting herself to this unnecessary stress. The problem was that the only Starbucks she knew of was several miles away, near a shopping center by Roxy's house, and she was driving now, in an unfamiliar and entirely residential area. She looked at her map and saw that she was near the first houses she had planned to see. Well, since she was there already, Anne decided, she might as well see them.

Inching along past gigantic Colonials and sprawling brick ranches, she had to admit that these houses were much too big, for just herself. She had told the real estate agent she had wanted someplace she could plant a garden, but this was ridiculous. Gallows Road, turn left, she remembered from the directions, and she turned, and found herself on a small, heavily wooded, two-lane street. Leaves covered the road, and vast oceans of leaves swelled in reddish-brown waves over the enormous yards facing the narrow road. She was amazed at the size of the yards—ahead, stood one of the houses on her list. It was a modern-looking structure, set back from the road, with a tall wall of windows. It was certainly impressive—especially the price it was selling for. No doubt, real estate here was more affordable than in California. Ogling the property, she was faintly aware of the sound of another car, approaching from the road she had just left. And then, in what seemed like the very next moment, the car was right behind her, following much too closely. She attempted to pull to the side, to let it pass, when she felt suddenly a sickening, dropping sensation in her stomach—the front of the sedan tipped forward and downwards. A deep ditch on the side of the road had been covered by leaves—this, her car had driven into. The car which she had let pass—a burgundy-colored, late-model sedan—drove by slowly, without stopping; the driver's face was a blank, white mass as it turned to look at her—she could not see the details of the face, and yet, it had been so near. Anne's hands began to shake, panicky thoughts seized her mind, and she felt like screaming, but slowly, with clenched teeth, she tried backing out of the ditch—with no success; the front wheels ground ineffectually against the sides of the ditch. And her mind was turning over and over as well, with so many questions—how could those people have just driven by like that? Surely it wouldn't have taken a minute or two to see if she was okay, or even to offer to phone for help! Of course, Anne had a cell phone – she was never without one—but still, the thought that someone could be so indifferent was infuriating and hateful. And after she had let them pass, too! Well, what was she going to do now? She could call roadside service, but by the time they got there, it would be too late to get Rachel. She could call Rachel's school and let them know she would be late. She could call Roxy. It would be all right. Still Anne couldn't stop shaking, and she got out of the car to see what there was to see. The ditch wasn't as deep as she thought—it was just enough so that her car could not get out. Really, all it needed was a good push from the front, and she'd be back on the road. She tried pushing the car for a few minutes, but it was like an ant trying to move a boulder. She uselessly got in and out of the car a few times, looked around quite thoroughly (there was no one around, despite all the houses), and resolved to call roadside services, when she heard another car approaching. Surely, this car would stop—she would make it stop. All she needed, she thought, was one more person, or two, to help push her car out of the ditch. She was someone who dreaded the thought of asking a stranger for help, much less frantically flagging one down—but she thought of little Rachel waiting for her, and she resolved to make a pathetic case of herself, if need be. The car was a gray SUV and it stopped; the driver was a young man in a barn coat, and she saw a small child in a car seat in the back.

"Could you please help me?" she pleaded. "I think I might be able to push my car out of there, with some help." And then she added, remembering her manners and the man's small child, despite her desperation. "If you have time."

But he said, "Sure", and there were so many grateful words tumbling around in her mind, trying to get out, that she was struck dumb.

The man parked his car, and came over to where her car lay, wedged into the ditch. They pushed and pushed, but it wasn't enough. The car would not budge.

He said, "I think we need more people". They looked around, but there was no one. Only leaves and trees and empty houses.

"If you need to go, I'll be fine," she said, near tears, but not willing to ask him to stay. "I do appreciate your trying to help."

The man looked embarrassed, and said no, he wasn't in any hurry. They just needed to find another person. He went back to his car, took out the car seat, with his son still strapped in, and set the child down, with the car seat, on the lawn. The child was about the same age as Rachel, with large, gray eyes and a big head of light-brown curls; he stared at Anne silently, seriously, and did not complain or cry. She wanted to make some comment about the child— about how well-behaved he was, and if he would be all right, sitting there, like that—and she would have liked to say something directly to the boy; of course, in a normal situation, she would have done all this. But today, her mind was frozen, and she could barely think, much less speak. Running continually in the back of her mind were images of poor Rachel, set upon the doorstep of the locked school, crying and wondering where her Grandma Anne was. She would never be able to get to the school before two or three, at this rate. And on top of that, she had wrecked Roxy's car. Anne was miserable and about to urge the man to go, tell him there was nothing more he could do, when once again, there was the sound of a vehicle, coming down the road. The young man said, "Here's somebody."

A large, rusty, blue truck came down the road, and the man driving it—a robust, white-haired, pink-cheeked, square-jawed, Southern type, if there ever was one, about sixty or maybe older, wearing a red, plaid, flannel shirt—looked over suspiciously at them, but he stopped; the young man in the barn coat took charge and asked the driver if he had some cables they could use to pull the car out with. She had not heard him mentioning that as a possibility before, but nothing could surprise her now.

Anne, of course, did not believe in miracles, and had once gotten upset when a classmate of Roxy's had sneered at her daughter, calling her "stupid", for not knowing what the Miracles were, but what came along next was about as close to a miracle as Anne had ever believed in. The tough-looking Southerner got out of his Ford, and retrieved from the back of the truck, what (Anne assumed) were a complicated set of cables. He silently, steadily, and expertly, worked to hook the cables up to Anne's car, and then, to the truck. The young man and Anne and the child looked on solemnly, and once Anne tried to thank the older man, but he ignored her and went on doing whatever he was doing, and the words stuck in her throat, and she had to keep them there, for a while. Finally, after the older man had carefully checked everything, he got into his truck, turned it on, drove forward, and pulled her car out of the ditch as if it had been a toy. Anne, on the other hand, was nearly weeping with anxiety, at this point, but she managed to pull herself together, and the young man suggested that she try to start the car. She got into her car, stuck the key into the ignition, and turned it, but to her horror, the engine made no sound. She tried again and again, with no results. She was dumbfounded, terror-stricken—after all that, and her car wouldn't start. She hurried out of the car, over to the older man, who was observing her, and held out her keys to him.

"I can't get it to start," she said. For a moment, no one moved or spoke (or laughed), and then the man took the keys without a word, got into her car, and started the engine on the first try. Anne's hand shook as she took back her keys. "Thank you, "she said. "I don't know what happened."

For the first time, she saw a small smile on his face, and he said, not unkindly, "You're just nervous."

"Yes, yes, I am," she said. "That's it. That's just it. I don't know what I would have done if you hadn't come along. I am so grateful to the both of you." She shook the young man's hand, and then she stuck out her hand towards the older man, and he shook it, too—but reluctantly, as if he was startled. Anne, however, was beyond caring about manners and propriety and rules and customs, because she was so glad, just so glad that these particular people had been here today, that they had chosen to do what they did, so glad it was all over now, and that she would be seeing her granddaughter soon. Then a thought startled her, and she added, "Please, can I give you something for your trouble?" She was low on cash that day, but she would give them whatever she had. That would be the solitary twenty-dollar bill in her purse. But the older man shook his head, and gave her his first real smile, a wide, genuine, toothy smile, and then she looked, truly looked at his face, something that most people don't often do, she realized—to look at another person's face. She saw intelligent, unwavering, bright-blue eyes, surrounded by a map of deep wrinkles, a large, proud nose that looked as if it might have been broken a few times, a square, probably usually grim mouth, surrounded by more deep wrinkles; he looked like someone important, maybe a general, or a president or a judge or someone along those lines—but no. That wasn't right. It was more than that, she thought, he looks normal, like what a normal man should look like. Yet, she knew that this man was from a vastly different world from hers, a world she never most likely, and unless with great effort on both sides, could ever be a part of, and she knew they would never be great, close friends, in any deep sense—much like she could never be friends with many of her kin and family, either, for that matter—and nor would they ever probably cross each other's paths again. Maybe this man might never have even stopped, if it hadn't been for the younger man. But nevertheless, she felt as if something had been changed for her—for him, too, perhaps—not just by his simple act of humanity, but also by her grateful recognition of it. And then the older man said, before driving away, "God bless you" and Anne understood, and even though she had long ago stopped believing in God, it was still one of nicest things anyone had ever said to her.

About the Author

Margaret F. Chen is the author of *Three Terrible Tales*. Her short stories and articles have appeared in many literary jounrals and magazines. She has lived in the suburbs Morgantown, West Virginia; Asheville, North Carolina; southeast and central Iowa; Minneapolis, Minnesota; Orange County, California; San Diego, California, and Washington D.C.